GOOSEBUMPS®
NOW WITH BONUS FEATURES!

THE WIZARD OF OOZE

R.L. STINE

SCHOLASTIC

Scholastic Children's Books
A division of Scholastic Ltd
Euston House, 24 Eversholt Street
London, NW1 1DB, UK
Registered office: Westfield Road, Southam, Warwickshire, CV47 0RA
SCHOLASTIC, GOOSEBUMPS, GOOSEBUMPS HORRORLAND, and
associated logos
are trademarks and/or registered trademarks of Scholastic Inc.

First published in the US by Scholastic Inc, 2010
This edition published in the UK by Scholastic Ltd, 2010
Goosebumps series created by Parachute Press, Inc.

Copyright © Scholastic Inc, 2010
The right of R.L. Stine to be identified as the author of this work
has been asserted by him.

ISBN 978 1407 11638 9

British Library Cataloguing-in-Publication Data.
A CIP catalogue record for this book is available from the British Library.

Printed in the UK by CPI Bookmarque, Croydon.
Papers used by Scholastic Children's Books are made from wood grown in
sustainable forests.

1 3 5 7 9 10 8 6 4 2

www.scholastic.co.uk/zone

MEET JONATHAN CHILLER. . .

He owns Chiller House, the HorrorLand gift shop. Sometimes he doesn't let kids pay for their souvenirs. Chiller tells them, "You can pay me *next time.*"

What does he mean by *next time*? What is Chiller's big plan?

Go ahead — the gates are opening. Enter HorrorLand. This time you might be permitted to leave . . . but for how long? Jonathan Chiller is waiting — to make sure you TAKE A LITTLE HORROR HOME WITH YOU!

PART ONE

Gabriella and I stopped in front of the carnival game booths. I read the big green-and-purple sign: THE PLAY PEN. IT'S NOT HOW MUCH YOU WIN OR LOSE BUT HOW MUCH YOU SCREAM YOUR HEAD OFF!

I rubbed my hands together. "These games look awesome," I said. "Maybe we'll win some cool prizes."

Gabriella tossed back her wavy black hair. "When I was little, I won a goldfish at a carnival," she said. "It was in a plastic bag filled with water. It was totally gross."

I squinted at her. "Totally gross?"

She nodded. "When I carried it into the house, the bag broke open. The goldfish and all the water gushed out, and my dog swallowed the fish. I cried for hours."

"You always were a big crybaby," I said.

"Was not!" She gave me a hard push, and I

3

stumbled into the PLAY PEN sign.

I rubbed my shoulder. "Pick on someone your own size," I said.

She's seven centimetres shorter than me. But she's tough and likes to punch and shove a lot.

We've been friends since first grade. But people think we're brother and sister because we look so much alike. We both have slender, serious faces, black hair and dark eyes.

My name is Marco Gonzalez, and she is Gabriella Grant. I guess we became friends because they made us sit alphabetically in first grade. We are both twelve. But everyone says I look older and more mature than she does. I'm not bragging. It's just true.

My parents drove us to HorrorLand for a vacation. After the first day, they let us wander off on our own. It's an OK place. Gabriella likes all the scary stuff. I'm into superheroes more than horror. Doctor Shark-Tooth, Coyote Boy-X and The Ooze are my favourites.

Gabriella gave my arm a hard pull. "Let's go on some rides, Marco."

"No, I want to play carnival games," I said. "I want to win a prize. I promised Zeke I'd bring him home something. Poor guy had such a bad cold, he had to stay home with Grandma."

"Your little brother was way angry," Gabriella said. "He really wanted to come with us."

"Zeke is *always* angry," I said. "Didn't you notice? He gets angry if his toast is too crumbly. *Angry* is his thing. Mum and Dad think it's adorable. He's a total pain."

Gabriella grinned. "Is that why you give him piggyback rides all the way to school?"

I rolled my eyes. "If I didn't carry him, he'd make me late every morning."

Her grin grew wider. "I know what you do, Marco. You put Zeke on your shoulders and pretend you're a superhero, flying him to school."

"That's a total lie," I said. I could feel my face grow hot. I knew I was blushing.

I turned away from her. A Horror waved to me from behind an ice cream cart. The Horrors are big, furry, green-and-purple characters. They are the guides and helpers who work at HorrorLand.

"Try our special flavour today?" the Horror called.

"What flavour?" I asked.

"Cookies 'n' Cow Brains," he replied. He held out an empty cone. "I've also got Chocolate Chip Toilet Bowl Cleaner."

"Uh . . . no thanks," I said.

It was a clear, cool night. A tiny sliver of a moon hung low in the sky. People crowded around the game booths. I heard a balloon pop. A few seconds later, a kid started to cry.

Down the long row of games, a raspy-voiced Horror was shouting, "Who's a loser? Come on – try your luck. Who's our next loser?"

I stepped up to the first game booth. SKULL TOSS.

A big Horror in purple overalls leaned on the counter. Behind him, I could see a mountain of grinning human skulls. He shoved three eyeballs across the counter towards me. Actually, they were table-tennis balls painted to look like eyeballs.

Gabriella stepped up to the counter. "What do you have to do?" she asked the Horror.

"Toss an eyeball into an empty eye socket," he growled. "If the eyeball sticks, you win a fabulous prize you'll never forget. Three eyeballs for a dollar."

"A fabulous prize?" she asked.

"I'm lying about that part," the Horror said. "Wanna play?" He tapped the eyeballs on the counter.

I pulled two dollars from my pocket and handed them over. "We'll both play," I said.

Gabriella's first ball bounced off a skull's forehead with a *clonk*. Her second toss hit an open nose hole and bounced away. Her third toss missed the skulls and hit the canvas at the back of the booth.

"You lose," the Horror said.

6

I grabbed a table-tennis ball, pulled back my hand and tossed. "Yes!" I cried. The ball slapped into an open eye socket and *stuck*!

And then I gasped as the skull opened its jaws and let out a shrill scream!

I froze. I stared in shock as the skulls all started to move. Their jaws made disgusting clicking sounds. *Whoo! Whoooo!* Their breath made a whistling sound as it escaped their mouths. The air suddenly smelled sour.

The Horror uttered a cry and staggered back. His eyes went wide with fear. "No! Oh, no!" he wailed. "No! Did you wake the DEAD?"

Gabriella and I didn't have time to move. The Horror grabbed my wrist. "What did you do?" he demanded. "What did you *do*?"

And then he burst out laughing. The skulls all stopped clicking their jaws at once.

"It's a joke," the Horror said. He let go of my wrist.

"I knew that," I said. But my heart was still pounding.

"Funny," Gabriella said. "Does Marco win a prize?"

The Horror reached under the counter. He handed me a tiny grey piece of fur. It looked like a dead caterpillar. "Enjoy it!" he said.

I held it up to study it. "What is it?" I asked him.

"A deadly piranha fish," he said. "Careful. It bites!"

"This guy is a riot," Gabriella muttered under her breath. We turned and walked away. "You can't give that to Zeke. It's terrible."

I tossed it into a big rubbish bin. Some of the fur stuck to my fingers. I looked around. "What should we play next?"

Gabriella pointed to a crowded booth across the road. "How about Zombie Darts?"

We wandered closer. I could see blue-faced men and women staggering stiffly at the back of the booth. The zombies grunted and groaned as people tossed darts at them.

"That looks easy," I said. "Maybe—"

Suddenly, a man stepped in front of us. I almost walked right into him! He was tall and wide and had a broad black moustache on his round face.

He wore a tall red cap with the words *Play to Win*. His shirt had noughts-and-crosses games scrawled all over the front. He wore a chequerboard waistcoat. His belt was made of playing cards.

He leaned close to us and whispered. "Want to play the good stuff?"

"Excuse me?" I said.

"Tired of the baby games?" he asked. His dark eyes flashed. The big moustache twitched. "Want to play some *real* games? Have a little excitement?"

"Do they have better prizes?" Gabriella asked him.

He nodded. "Good games. Good prizes," he said. He seemed tense. He glanced all around as if he was being followed. I saw droplets of sweat on his forehead.

"Who are you?" I asked.

He adjusted his playing-card belt. "My name is Winner. Winner Taikall. I'm the Games Master. I'll take you to the *good* games."

I turned to Gabriella. "Should we check this out?" I whispered.

She shrugged.

"Everyone wins – nobody loses . . . much!" Winner exclaimed. "Remember, a winner never quits, and a quitter never survives!"

Survives?

"You're joking, right?" Gabriella asked him.

"Of course I'm joking," he replied. "Follow me." His stomach bounced in front of him as he walked. He kept glancing behind him to make sure we were following.

He led us along the brick wall at the back of the carnival games. Then we followed him to a little black door cut into the wall. The doorway was low. We had to duck our heads as we stepped inside.

Our shoes scraped the earthen floor as we walked through a long, dimly lit tunnel. The air grew colder. The tunnel dipped downhill. Was he taking us underground?

"Where are we going?" I asked. My voice sounded hollow. It echoed off the tunnel walls.

"To my special games room," Winner replied. "You can't lose! After all, my name is Winner!"

The tunnel grew narrower. He had to turn sideways to squeeze through.

His moustache twitched as he grinned at us. "I like all kinds of games," he said. "Even dangerous games. How about you?"

Dangerous games?

I grabbed Gabriella's arm. "I don't like this," I whispered. "Are we making a *big* mistake?"

We followed the big man out of the tunnel. Bright yellow light poured over us.

I blinked, waiting for my eyes to adjust. We were standing in the middle of a big square room. The walls were covered with games boards. He led us up to a red curtain at the back.

"This is my private games room," Winner said. "I promise you will have an exciting time. And yes, my prizes are better than the Play Pen prizes."

His smile faded. "That's because you have to *earn* them!"

I felt a chill run down my back. What exactly did he mean by that? Why were we the only ones in this games room?

I turned to Gabriella. I couldn't tell if she was as worried as I was. She likes to play tough. She never lets anyone know if she's scared or tense.

"What game are we going to play?" she asked Winner.

"It's a mystery tug-of-war," he said. He parted the curtain and bent down, searching for something behind it.

"Why is it a mystery?" Gabriella demanded.

He chuckled. "It wouldn't be a mystery if I told you – would it?"

He pulled out a fat rope from behind the red curtain. It was tightly coiled. He started to unroll it.

"This is going to be the most exciting tug-of-war game ever!" he declared. He stretched out one end of the rope. "Go ahead. Grab it."

I pulled the rope towards me. Gabriella and I took hold of the end.

"I don't have to explain the rules to you," Winner said. He kept unrolling the rope. "Tug with all your might. Pull the rope to you – and you can't lose!"

"Who are we playing against?" I asked.

Winner didn't answer. He carried the other end of the rope with him and disappeared behind the closed curtain.

"This is weird," Gabriella muttered.

"It's HorrorLand," I said. "It's *supposed* to be weird. And a little scary."

"We should have asked him what the prize is," she said.

"Roll the dice!" Winner called from the other side of the curtain. "Spin the wheel! Push START.

Game on! Game on! Get ready to play!"

Gabriella moved in front of me and wrapped the end of the rope around her wrist. I grabbed the rope with both hands and braced myself. I bent my knees and tightened my leg muscles, getting ready to tug.

"OK . . . START!" Winner shouted.

I felt a strong pull on the rope. I gripped it tighter and pulled back.

"Hey!" Gabriella let out a shout as the rope slipped out of her grasp. She grabbed it again and leaned back against me as we both pulled.

We leaned way back and gave a hard pull. The rope moved towards us. Then it was jerked back hard.

I stared at the red curtain. Who was on the other side? Who were Gabriella and I playing against?

Someone very strong, I decided. We were being pulled forward. Centimetre by centimetre, we were being tugged closer to the curtain.

"Pull hard! Pull hard!" Gabriella shouted.

"What do you think I'm doing?" I cried.

I dug my shoes into the floor and leaned all the way back. And pulled. Pulled with all my strength.

"*Ow!*" The rope jerked hard and burned the skin on my palms.

Gabriella and I stumbled forwards. Another hard tug, and we were almost to the curtain.

"We're losing!" Gabriella cried. "Marco – pull harder!"

But then we both cried out as the curtain slid open. And we saw who we were playing against.

No one!

There was no one on the other end of the rope!

Another hard tug jerked us forwards.

"Keep pulling! Don't give up! Keep pulling!" Winner shouted from somewhere behind us.

"But there's *no one there*!" I cried.

The other end of the rope floated in mid-air. The players on the other side were *invisible*!

But that was impossible. Wasn't it?

We were being pulled through the open curtain. About to lose this crazy tug-of-war.

My hands burned. My arms ached. My heart throbbed in my chest.

"Don't give up!" Winner shouted.

"OK, OK. One last try," I murmured to Gabriella. My voice came out in a breathless whisper. "On three, OK?"

I dug my heels into the floor. I gripped the rope tighter.

"One . . . two . . ."

I didn't make it to three.

Because the rope wiggled in my hand. I felt it change. I felt it grow smooth against my burning skin. Smooth and dry.

The rope changed.

Warm and dry and soft.

I saw black eyes stare at me. A narrow jaw worked up and down.

A soft *hissssss* rang in my ears.

A snake! I was gripping a snake! My hands were wrapped around its head!

I was tugging on a two-metre-long snake, its jaws hissing and snapping.

"Nooooo!"

I uttered a scream of horror and pain as it sank its fangs deep into my wrist.

Gabriella and I staggered back. The big snake snapped out of our hands. It hit the floor and wriggled towards the curtain.

I grabbed my wrist and raised it to my face. "Ohhhh." I saw two round, red fang marks in the skin.

I suddenly felt faint. Dizzy.

I spun around, searching for Winner. "What kind of *game* is this?" I cried. "The snake – it *bit* me! Is it poisonous? *Is* it?"

No sign of him.

I studied my wrist again. "Hey – wait!" The fang marks had vanished. Completely disappeared.

Was the snake some kind of fake? Was it all a trick?

"L-let's get out of here," I stammered.

Gabriella and I turned. Winner stood behind us at the doorway. He had a pleased grin under his moustache. He strode quickly towards us.

I pointed back to the snake. "How did you do that?" I cried.

"Who was pulling the rope?" Gabriella asked.

"How did you change it into a snake?"

"Is it really alive?"

We bombarded him with questions.

Winner motioned with both hands for us to stop. "You just have to know how to play the game," he said. "So sorry you didn't win."

"But – how could we win?" I cried. "Our opponents were invisible! And the rope turned into a huge snake!"

Winner's eyes narrowed at me. "Are you saying it wasn't a fair game?"

"I didn't say that," I replied. "It's just that—"

"So . . . we don't win anything?" Gabriella said.

"Every player is a winner!" he exclaimed. "Every winner is a player! Every loser is a winner! And every prize is a prize worth winning!"

"He's crazy!" I whispered.

"So does that mean we do or we don't win a prize?" Gabriella was not ready to give up.

Winner reached into a pocket of his chequerboard waistcoat. "I have a consolation prize for you," he said. He pulled out a small square of paper and handed it to me.

I unfolded it and read the black words against the green background. It said:

10% Discount Coupon
Any Item at CHILLER HOUSE

"Game over," Winner said. He made a shooing motion towards the tunnel opening. "Three strikes and you're out." He stepped in front of me and brought his face close to mine. "Unless you'd like *sudden-death overtime*?"

I backed away. "Sudden death? Uh ... no thanks. Guess Gabriella and I will go now."

We started into the tunnel. I glanced back and saw Winner lift the big snake from the floor. He began to coil it around his hand.

Was it a rope again? Was the whole thing some kind of magic trick?

Gabriella tugged my hand. "Come on. Let's get out of here."

We made our way through the twisting, cold tunnel. It was a steep climb going this direction. We were out of breath by the time we stepped through the little black door and back into the park.

We walked along the brick wall. The Play Pen game booths were as crowded as ever.

"What do you want to play next?" Gabriella said. I think she was joking.

"That's enough for now," I said. I turned back towards the tunnel. "Hey – look!" I grabbed Gabriella by the shoulders and turned her around.

"What's your problem?" she snapped.

"The black door," I said. "Look. It's gone."

We ran back to the wall where the door had stood. I ran my hand along it.

Solid brick.

A tall Horror in a black-and-orange Monster Police uniform came striding past us. His orange cape fluttered behind him.

Gabriella grabbed his arm. "Can you help us?" she asked.

The Horror tilted back his black cap. He had small curved horns poking up from the top of his head. "What's up?" he growled.

"Well . . ." Gabriella began, "we were just back there with the Games Master but . . ."

He rubbed one horn with two fingers. "Who?"

"You know," Gabriella said. "Winner Taikall. The Games Master."

The Horror burst out laughing. "Winner take all? That's funny."

"No. Really," Gabriella insisted.

The tall Horror squinted down at her. "Someone was playing a joke on you," he growled. "There's no Games Master at HorrorLand."

The Chiller House shop looked like a little house. It was at the end of a row of shops at the back of Zombie Plaza. The shop had a brightly lit front window filled with funny souvenirs.

A sign above the entrance read: SHOP TILL YOU DROP (REALLY!). The straw welcome mat in front of the door said: GO AWAY.

"Maybe we can find something for Zeke in here," I said. I pulled open the door.

A long aisle stretched down the centre of the shop. On both sides, tall shelves and glass cases were jammed with weird, funny items. Skulls hung from the ceiling. Stuffed monsters were piled on the floor.

I picked up a small box from the first counter. "Maybe Zeke would like this," I said.

Gabriella took it from me. "Huh? Why would he like a bar of soap?"

Then she read the label: FLESH-EATING SOAP.

"When you wash with it, it eats your skin away," I said.

We both laughed. Gabriella pointed to an item next to the soap. A human hand cut off at the wrist. "It looks so real," she said. "It must be made of rubber."

She reached for it – and the fingers wrapped around her wrist.

Gabriella screamed in surprise. "Marco – help me!"

I prised the fingers open and tugged the hand off her. "It must be electronic or something," I said. "But it feels like real skin. Yuck."

"Here's something Zeke would totally like," I said. I held it up to Gabriella. EXTRA NOSE. "See? It's a fake nose. The back is sticky. You stick it to your forehead and freak out your friends."

"Awesome," she said.

"Do you like that nose?" a voice asked. "I have it in three sizes."

I turned and saw an old man at the front counter. He was bald and red-faced. He had small square glasses perched on the end of his long, pointed nose.

He wore an old-fashioned brown suit and waistcoat with a ruffled shirt. He made me think of the painting of Ben Franklin in one of my school books.

He came shuffling up to us with his hands clasped in front of him. "I am Jonathan Chiller," he said. "Welcome to Chiller House." When he smiled, a gold tooth gleamed in the side of his mouth.

"Extra Nose is very popular," he said. "And here's something new I just got this week." He held up a small box: DO-IT-YOURSELF DENTIST KIT.

"It has stickers you put on your teeth," he explained. "It makes it look like you've got ugly brown stains and big holes in your teeth."

Gabriella laughed. "Excellent!"

Chiller said something else. But I didn't hear him. I'd spotted something very interesting. I pulled it off the shelf. My heart started to race as I flipped through it.

A graphic novel. About The Ooze. My favourite comic villain. A graphic novel I'd never seen before!

"I don't believe it!" I cried. I shoved the cover into Gabriella's face. "Look! I don't have this one!"

She read the title out loud. "*The Wizard of Ooze.*

"Marco – you *must* have read it," she said. "I know you've read every comic and graphic novel there is about The Ooze. You're *obsessed*!"

My hands were actually shaking. She's right – I'm obsessed. I've read every Ooze book there is. Sometimes I make up my own stories about him.

And OK, I admit it. Sometimes I stand in front of the mirror with a sneer on my face, and I repeat The Ooze's most famous phrase: *"Know what I mean?"*

"Know what I mean?"

"Know what I mean?"

I can sound pretty tough when I want to.

"You sure you don't have this book?" Gabriella said. She turned to Chiller. "You should see Marco's collection. It takes up a whole wall!"

Chiller took the book from my hands. He gazed through his square glasses at the cover. "This is a very limited edition," he said. "It has the original story in it. The very beginning of The Ooze."

He tapped the cover. "And in the back, there's a special bonus section. It tells step-by-step how you can become a superhero."

I laughed and rolled my eyes. "Yeah, sure. And then I could battle The Ooze!"

Gabriella gave me a shove. "You would *love* being a superhero, and you know it."

"Well, it's not going to happen from a comic book," I said. "But I have to buy this. I need it for my collection. And I'll buy an Extra Nose for my brother."

"Very good," Chiller said. "Follow me."

He led us up to the front counter. He pulled supplies from a drawer. Then he carefully wrapped the nose and the book in grey wrapping paper.

I reached into my jeans pocket for my money. "How much is it?" I asked. "I was so excited, I forgot to look at the price."

Chiller motioned for me to put my money back. "You don't have to pay me now," he said. His gold tooth gleamed as he smiled. "You can pay me next time."

Huh? Next time?

He tied a dark red ribbon around the wrapped package. Then he pulled something from the drawer and tucked it into the ribbon.

I stared at it. A little figure. A tiny Horror, like the ones who worked at HorrorLand.

Jonathan Chiller's smile grew wider as he handed the package to me. "Here you are," he said. "Take a little Horror home with you!"

PART TWO

On the car ride home, Gabriella and I sat silently
in the back seat. I had my face buried in the Ooze
book. Gabriella read over my shoulder.

"Look at those unusual trees," Mum said from
the passenger seat up front. "Have you ever seen
anything like those?"

Gabriella and I didn't raise our heads from the
book. "Awesome," I said.

"The trees?" Mum asked.

"No. The Ooze," I muttered. "He has to be the
coolest ever. I mean, a villain made entirely out
of oil sludge? How cool is that?"

"Well . . . he's definitely yucky and oily and
gross," Gabriella said.

"I can't believe you kids are missing all this
beautiful scenery," Mum said.

"I don't get it," Gabriella said. "He's just a
huge pile of disgusting gunk. Why do you like
him so much?"

"That's why," I said.

"Horse farm to your left," Dad said, slowing the car. "Look on the hill. Those horses are definitely thoroughbreds. Wonder if they race."

Gabriella tried to take the book from me. But I held on to it. "I'm not finished," I said. "You don't like it anyway."

Gabriella made a pouty face. "There's nothing else to do. I accidentally packed away my iPod."

"You could look at the wonderful scenery," Mum said.

"Did you see the bonus section about how to become a superhero?" I asked Gabriella.

"Not yet. You're hogging the book."

"It says it's easy to find the superhero inside you."

Gabriella laughed. "You mean you changed your mind about it? Now you think this comic book could actually turn you into a superhero?"

"Well . . . not really," I said.

"You know why they put that stuff in the back of graphic novels," Gabriella said. "It's just there to fill up the pages. The story ended. So they have to put a lot of other junk back there. *No way* it's going to turn you into a superhero."

"You're right," I said. "You're definitely right."

"Give me a turn," Gabriella said. She tried to pull the book from my hands again – and something fell on to the car seat.

She picked it up. "Check it out. A bookmark." She studied it. "Totally weird."

"Why?" I asked. "What does it say?"

"I can't read it," she said. "It's in a foreign language."

I grabbed the bookmark and tucked it back inside the book. "We can study it later," I said. "This book is definitely *awesome*."

"Look at that up ahead – an entire herd of black sheep!" Dad said.

We dropped Gabriella off at her house. Then as we pulled up our driveway, Zeke came running out to greet us. Of course, the first thing he said to me was – "What did you bring me?"

I helped Mum and Dad carry in the suitcases. Then I gave Zeke his Extra Nose.

The kid is so weird. He stuck it on the living room wall – not on his face. He thought that was a riot.

I spent the rest of the day helping Mum unpack and getting my room back together. We were all tired from the long car trip and went to bed pretty early.

I kept thinking about The Ooze and superpowers . . . superpowers. . .

I yawned. I was too tired to read. But tomorrow I would definitely try to find mine.

The next day was Saturday. That afternoon, I was upstairs in my room. I had the Ooze book open on my bed. I kept flipping through the pages in the back.

Find Your Inner Superhero

That's what it said. Of course, I knew the whole idea was crazy. Totally dumb. No way it could work.

No way.

But I still wanted to try it. I *had* to try it.

Sprawled on my stomach on the bed, I turned to the first instruction page and started to read...

There are many powers to choose from. You must explore. You must experiment. It is the only way to find the power that you were born to use. When you find your power, you will KNOW it. Your power will stay with you. It will BECOME you – and you will become IT!

Wow. Marco, you can do this! I told myself. *Go ahead, dude. Give it a try!*

Is your inner superpower the ability to fly?
To find out, you must concentrate ... concen-
trate your thoughts and your muscles. Flight
is the gift of birds. To begin, you will need to
borrow from the birds. You will need two fresh
bird feathers, still warm from the bird's liv-
ing body. . . .

Two bird feathers.

"No problem," I murmured to myself.

Most people would have trouble finding fresh,
warm bird feathers. But not me. Maybe that
meant I was destined to fly.

I left the book open on the bed. I pulled on my
trainers and made my way out into the hall.

Zeke's room is opposite mine. I saw him in
there sticking the Extra Nose on to his laptop
screen. "Where are you going?" he called.

"Outside for a minute," I said.

"Want to play tetherball with me?" Zeke

33

asked. "Dad fixed the rope."

"I'm busy," I told him.

"Busy being a jerk," he said.

Typical.

I stepped out the back door. It was a steamy, grey day. Dark clouds hung low over the trees. It looked like it might rain later.

Mr Clare, our neighbour, has a pigeon coop behind his garage. He keeps dozens of pigeons. I could hear them cooing.

I checked to make sure he wasn't around. The back of his house was dark. His car wasn't in the driveway.

Mr Clare doesn't like me. It's because he thinks I was responsible for a bunch of kids running over his tomato plants. It's true we were there, searching for our frisbee. But we didn't exactly *run* over the plants.

Anyway, he definitely wouldn't like me plucking his pigeons. If he caught me, how could I explain what I was doing?

I ducked behind the low bushes between our gardens. And I ran as fast as I could to the pigeon cages. They were stacked high against the garage. I counted six wooden cages with maybe ten or twelve birds in a cage.

As I ran up to them, the pigeons began to cluck and flap their wings and knock each other off their perches. "*Ssshhh.* Quiet, guys,"

34

I whispered.

I glanced around the garage to the house. Did a light go on in Mr Clare's back window?

My heart started to pound. My mouth was suddenly as dry as sand.

The stupid pigeons were squawking like chickens! They flapped their wings loudly. Two of them started fighting, pecking at each other's eyes.

I tried to reach my fingers into the middle cage. But the chicken wire was too tight. No way I could pluck two feathers, even if a pigeon stood still for me.

I reached for the latch on the cage door. The pigeons started *hoo-hoo-hoo*ing louder.

"*Shhhh*. Quiet, guys. Please!"

I peeked again around the corner of the garage wall. Yes. I definitely saw a light in the kitchen. And was that Mr Clare peering out the window?

I had to act fast. My hand trembled as I pushed down the latch. I pulled open the cage door.

"Hey!"

Pigeons flapped and fluttered to the opening. They pushed against my hand, eager to escape.

"Who is back there?" I heard Mr Clare's shout from the house. "Is somebody back there?"

A pigeon slid past my hand and almost

squeezed out of the cage. I kept the door pressed against my wrist. Pigeons squawked and jumped off their perches at me.

I grabbed at some tail feathers. Missed. Grabbed again.

Yes! I had three feathers pinched between my fingers. One more than I needed.

I squeezed them tightly, praying that they wouldn't fall out. And carefully, I slid my hand out of the cage. With my free hand, I closed the cage door and latched it.

I moved the feathers into my palm and wrapped my fingers around them to protect them. Then I took off, running on trembling legs.

I made it to the long row of bushes just as Mr Clare's back door swung open. I saw him step out of his house, tying the belt of his grey bathrobe.

"Who's back there?"

The pigeons squawked and cried in reply.

Hiding behind the bushes, I watched him stomp back to the pigeon cages. When he disappeared behind the garage, I took off running. I darted into the house and slammed the door behind me.

Dad was at the kitchen table, working on his laptop. He looked up and stared at my closed fist. "Marco, what have you got there?"

"Uh . . . something for a science experiment

for school," I said.

It wasn't a *total* lie. It *was* a science experiment.

I gripped the feathers tightly, keeping them warm. And I ran up the stairs to my room.

Zeke was in his room across the hall. I could hear the rattle of gunfire and the roar of exploding cannons. Zeke loves war video games.

I carried the feathers to my bed and set them down gently on the pillow. I took a deep breath. My heart was still racing.

I picked up the book and read more of the instructions. . .

You will need the two fresh, warm bird feathers and a packet of yeast. . .

Back to the kitchen. Dad was squinting at his screen. Concentrating hard.

"Do we have yeast?" I asked. "It's for that science experiment."

He didn't look up. Just pointed to the cabinet above the stove.

I fumbled around in there until I found a box of powdered yeast packets. I carried it up to my room and returned to the book. . .

The feathers will help you fly. The yeast will let you rise high. Place a feather in each pocket. Then pour the yeast on top of your head. Concentrate your powers. If the ability to fly is yours, you will take off instantly.

WARNING: Do not jump off a roof or out a high window until you learn if your inner superpower is flight.

Well, I knew the whole idea was weird. But I'd risked my life to get the pigeon feathers. I had to try it.

I shoved a feather into each of my jeans pockets. Then I opened the box and took out several packets of yeast and poured them on to my hair. Some of the yeast fell on to the shoulders of my T-shirt. I just left it there.

I pulled the desk chair out from in front of my computer and dragged it in to the middle of the room. Then I climbed on to it. Carefully . . . carefully so I wouldn't spill any more yeast.

I shut my eyes and tried to concentrate.

I knew this was totally crazy. But I felt excited. I took a deep breath and held it.

What if it worked? What if I really could fly like a superhero?

I concentrated . . . concentrated. . .

I opened my eyes. "Here goes!" I exclaimed out loud.

I bent my knees – and leaped off the chair.

Into the air. Yes! Yes!

I waited to land on the floor. But no – I floated . . . floated in the air.

I raised my arms and floated a little

higher. I was at least a metre above the floor!

It was crazy. It was *impossible*! But it was working.

I raised my hands higher and felt myself rise up. Like a feather in the wind. My body was swept up – until my hands touched the ceiling.

Then . . . "OH, NOOOOOOOO!"

A long moan escaped my throat as I plunged straight down.

I landed hard on my face. The air whooshed out of my lungs. I made a choking sound. I couldn't breathe. Waves of pain shot up and down my body.

"Ohh . . . help," I gasped. "Help me. I've broken every bone in my body!"

Slowly, I lifted my head. I took a deep, shuddering breath.

My chin felt wet. I wiped it with two fingers and saw bright red blood. I could taste the blood on my tongue.

I groaned and tried to sit up. My head throbbed. I tested my arms, my legs.

Nothing broken after all.

I looked up – and saw Zeke standing in my doorway. His eyes were wide with surprise. "Mum! Dad!" he shouted at the top of his lungs. "Marco has a bloody nose!"

Zeke jumped aside as Mum and Dad came thundering into the room. "What's going on?" Dad cried. He bent down to pull me to my feet.

Mum started dabbing at my nose with a tissue. "What did you do? Marco? Are you hurt? Why were you down on the floor?"

"I . . . uh. . ." The words caught in my throat.

"He fell off his chair," Zeke told them. "He was standing on his chair and he fell off it. And he landed on his face."

I stood there blinking, feeling wobbly. Zeke hadn't seen me fly. He only saw me fall.

Dad still had hold of my arm. "Did you deliberately jump off the chair?" he demanded. "You weren't pretending to be a superhero again – were you, Marco?"

"No way. Of course not," I insisted. I pressed the tissue to my nose. The nosebleed was stopping. "I . . . I told you. I was doing a science experiment. For extra credit."

They always liked it when I did things for extra credit.

"But what's this in your hair?" Mum asked. She shook her hand in my hair, and the powdery yeast came falling out.

"I think maybe I have dandruff," I said.

Dad nodded his head. "Ninety per cent of all accidents happen in the home," he said. "You have to remember that, Marco."

Dad is a total safety freak. He has a seat belt on his reclining lounge chair!

Mum and Dad questioned me for a few more minutes. They made me promise I'd try a science experiment that wasn't so dangerous. Then they went back downstairs.

Zeke sat on the edge of my bed. He had a

41

strange smile on his face. "Sure you don't want to play tetherball? I'll let you win!"

"Get out of my room," I growled. "Go on. Beat it, Zeke. And stop spying on me."

He kicked the desk chair and sent it rolling to the wall. Then he stomped back to his room.

I closed the door behind him. I still felt a little shaky. But I was totally excited.

It actually worked! I thought. *I really flew!*

True. It was only for about ten seconds. But I really did take off and fly up to the ceiling.

Why didn't it last longer?

I knew why. Flight was not my secret superpower.

The book said when I found my power, I would *know* it. It would stick with me.

I had to keep trying until I found the power hidden inside me.

I picked up the book and started turning pages.

Finding the SUPERSTRENGTH Within You. . .

Yes! Superstrength! I had a feeling *this* might be my secret power. I dropped on to my bed with the book in my lap and read the instructions.

If strength is your superpower, you can find it easily. You need to test yourself against the world's strongest substance. Nothing is stronger than clear plastic kitchen wrap. It will stretch but not tear.

Wrap your body from the chest down in an entire roll of clear plastic wrap. Make a cocoon of plastic wrap. But keep your arms free. Then concentrate ... concentrate. You will find the strength waiting to be discovered.

OK. This sounded easy. And Mum and Dad would definitely approve. No jumping off chairs.

Downstairs, I heard music in the den. Mum and Dad were in there, reading. I crept to the kitchen and borrowed a roll of plastic wrap from the kitchen pantry.

I grew more and more excited as I carried it to my room and started to unroll it. I wrapped myself in the clear plastic, legs first. When my legs were covered in a thick layer, I started wrapping my waist.

Making a plastic-wrap cocoon was harder than it sounds. As I raised it to my chest, my hands kept fumbling the roll. I dropped it and the sticky plastic stuck to the roll.

I finally managed to prise it apart. I wrapped my chest, then worked my way down. It took a long time. There are *miles* of plastic wrap on one roll!

Finally, there I was. A plastic-wrap mummy. The empty box fell to the floor. I couldn't walk. I couldn't move.

I felt sweat pour down my forehead and cheeks. It was HOT in there!

"Hope this works," I muttered. "If I don't have superstrength, I'll never get *out* of this!"

I shut my eyes and concentrated. I pictured bulging muscles. A weight lifter raising gigantic weights above his head.

Concentrate . . . concentrate. . .

Suddenly, I felt something. The plastic wrap squeaked. It squeaked as it stretched. I heard it rip along my legs.

The wrap tore apart at my chest. I heard another loud *rip* – looked down. My T-shirt had popped open.

The muscles on my arms bulged. They expanded like balloons. My T-shirt ripped totally apart. My jeans started to rip.

I could feel myself hulking up.

My whole body was growing . . . stretching . . . pulling against the plastic-wrap cocoon – until the plastic popped and fell away.

My chest roared out, shredding my T-shirt. My legs grew heavier . . . wider. . . My jeans popped open as my waist swelled – and then the jeans ripped to shreds.

How long would this go on? Was I going to grow and grow until I was as big as the house? What if it didn't stop?

Oh, wow. *What if it didn't stop?*

44

A few seconds later, I heard a *whoosh*. Like air escaping a balloon.

The room swung around me. I felt dizzy. The ceiling tilted over my head.

It took only a second or two. The whole room seemed to shoot out. Then the floor rose up to meet me. And I shrank back to my normal size.

"Ohhhh." I stood there shivering and shaking. The muscles in my arms and legs all quivered. My skin tingled. Everything itched and prickled and shook.

It worked! I thought. *How totally amazing! It worked.*

But again . . . for only about ten seconds.

I didn't move. I guess I was in shock or something.

It took me a while to realize that I had completely burst out of my clothes. I was standing there totally naked!

And then out in the hall, I heard Zeke shouting: "Mum! Dad! Marco is doing weird things up here! Come quick! Come quick!"

I had to put something on before they got up here.

I stumbled to the wardrobe. I tripped over my shredded jeans.

I could hear my parents' footsteps running up the stairs.

"Hurry!" Zeke was shouting to them. "I think Marco is in trouble again!"

The little snitch.

No time. No time.

I grabbed my pyjamas from the pile of dirty clothes on my floor.

"Marco was doing something weird!" Zeke said. The bedroom door started to swing open.

I scrambled into the pyjamas, gasping, my heart pounding.

I kicked the shredded jeans and T-shirt under the bed as Mum burst into the room. She glanced all around.

Dad followed, a stern expression on his face. "Marco, what's up this time?" he demanded.

Mum frowned at me. "Why are you wearing pyjamas in the middle of the day? Are you feeling ill?"

"N-no," I stammered. "I just wanted to be comfortable." Lame. But it was the best I could do.

They both stared hard at me. Behind them in the doorway, that brat Zeke had his arms crossed in front of him. A big grin on his face. "He was doing something crazy in here. I heard him."

Mum gazed at the Ooze book on my bed. "Are you still reading that comic book? Why don't you go outside and get some fresh air?"

"Well ... I'm kinda busy in here," I said. "Maybe later."

"He won't play with me," Zeke whined.

It took a while longer to get them all out of my room. I couldn't shake off the trembly feeling. My skin still itched and tingled.

I stared at the Ooze book on the bed. Should I try one more superpower?

I'd tried two powers and both were not for me. Maybe if I tried a third...

Then I had a sad thought: *What if none of them work for me? What if I don't have any superpowers?*

What if I'm just a normal kid, not special at all?

I had to keep trying. I picked up the book.

Which power should I choose? It had to be a water power. I love to swim. I'm a good diver, too. It had to be a water power. Yes! Yes!

This time, I *knew* it would work!

10

The phone rang.

Startled, I dropped the book on to the floor. I clicked open my phone.

"Marco? What's up?"

"Oh, hi, Gabriella," I said into the phone. "Not much."

I couldn't tell her about my adventures with the Ooze book. She'd either laugh at me and call me a liar, or she'd want to come over and try to be a superhero, too!

"Didn't you forget about something?" she asked. She didn't wait for me to answer. "The comic book convention downtown?"

"Oh, no! Oh, wow!" I cried. "What time is it? Are we too late?"

How could I forget the comic book convention? It's the most awesome day of the year for me.

The huge convention centre was always mobbed with comic book fans. Every publisher had big displays. Dozens of artists and comic book writers were there. People walked around in superhero and supervillain costumes. Thousands of comics for sale.

"Are we going?" Gabriella asked.

"Of course," I said. "Meet me at the bus stop in ten minutes." I clicked the phone shut.

I started for the door. *Oh, wait.* I was still in my pyjamas.

I pulled on a fresh pair of jeans and a T-shirt. Grabbed a wad of money from my secret hiding place at the back of my sock drawer. And hurried out of my room.

Zeke blocked my way to the stairs. "Can I come, too?"

"You were spying again?" I asked. "No way. You're not coming."

"Take me with you," he insisted. He wrapped his arms around my waist and squeezed tight. "I won't let go unless you take me."

I prised him off me. "No. Beat it."

"But you get to go everywhere!" he cried. "I don't get to go anywhere!"

"That's because you're a shrimp," I said. "Maybe when I get back, I'll play tetherball with you."

"I don't want to," Zeke growled. He kicked me hard in the ankle and stomped into his room.

The convention centre is a huge glass building that stretches for three or four city blocks. Gabriella and I bought our tickets and stepped into the enormous exhibition hall.

Every aisle was jammed with people. Awesome displays and booths and video screens and tall billboards and signs stretched as far as I could see. Voices rang out in an excited roar. Music blared.

It was too much to see and hear. I wanted to spend a *week* there!

We pushed our way through the video games section. Hundreds of people jammed the booths, testing out new games and game systems.

I stopped and watched a bunch of girls playing a 3-D battle game called *Princess Wars*. Princesses in long white gowns were swinging battleaxes, trying to knock the tiaras off each other's heads.

Gabriella and I turned a corner and bumped right into Cucumber and his sidekick, Carrot-Stick. They are the most popular members of the Salad League of Mutants. Some little kids were waving autograph books, trying to get the Vegetables of Iron to sign them.

We turned down another aisle. A man dressed as a dollar sign stood on a platform, laughing like a maniac and tossing piles of fake money into the air. He kept pointing to a green-and-white sign: CRAZY, INSANE PRICES PAID FOR YOUR COMIC COLLECTION.

"That reminds me," Gabriella said. She bumped into me as a group of kids tore past. "Did you try any of those tests in your Ooze book? You know. About finding your superpowers?"

I was tempted to tell her the truth. But I knew it would only get me into trouble.

"No. You were right about those chapters," I said. "They're just filler. It's a big fake. Forget about it."

She studied me for a moment. Maybe she knew that I wasn't exactly telling the truth.

The aisles got more crowded as we came near the comic book section. I passed a table of Louie Kablooey bobblehead dolls. Louie Kablooey has a very interesting superpower. He can blow himself to smithereens, like a bomb.

"They should make these bobblehead dolls explode when you shake them," Gabriella said. "That would be way cool."

"Hey, check it out!" I pointed to the end of the aisle. A big sign stretched across the back wall. Huge black oily letters spelled out **OOZE**. The word dripped down like an oil spill.

The Ooze display booth had to be a *block long*. Video screens showed preview scenes from next summer's Ooze movie. Giant cut outs of The Ooze towered over both ends of the display. A wall of shelves held all the Ooze books, comics, games and DVDs.

The booth was jammed with Ooze fans. It took Gabriella and me a long time to push our way to the front.

I watched part of the movie preview on a big video screen. In the movie, The Ooze poured himself over a group of helpless policemen. He became a tidal wave of gunk. The special effects were awesome!

I gazed down from the screen. I was standing in front of a table filled with Ooze products. "Sweet!" I cried. I studied the Ooze lunch boxes, trainers, sweets, posters. I picked up a box of Ooze Yoghurt.

"Have you tried it, sonny?" a man asked. "Tastes like liquorice. Feels like Ooze."

"Cool," I said.

The man nodded. He was lanky and thin. He had a red face, bright green eyes, and red hair tied behind his head in a ponytail.

He was dressed in a grey oil company uniform, with the word *Ooze* dripping on his pocket in red letters. His name badge said his name was Sammy.

"Sonny, have you seen the Ooze iPod holder?" he asked. He held one up. "It's really made of ooze."

Gabriella elbowed me. "Check out the graphic novels, Marco. I think they have them all."

I turned and gazed at a wall of graphic novels. The Ooze stared out from every cover. My eyes went up and down the rows of books. I had every one of them at home.

I turned to Gabriella. "I don't see *The Wizard of Ooze*," I said. "That's the only one that's missing."

Suddenly, a hand grabbed my shoulder. Sammy narrowed his green eyes at me. "Come with me," he said. "Now."

He started to drag me away.

"What's wrong?" I asked. "What did I do?"

Sammy dragged me past a display of Ooze toothbrushes. They were definitely cool. The handles looked like dripping ooze. And they came with a tube of black Ooze toothpaste.

He didn't say a word until we were at the back corner of the booth. "I just want to have a little talk," he said. "Did I hear you mention *The Wizard of Ooze* graphic novel?"

I nodded. "Yeah. It wasn't in the display."

He brushed a hand back through his fiery red hair and squinted at me. "Have you ever seen it, sonny?"

"I *have* it," I said. "I bought a copy."

He sucked in his breath. His eyes went wide.

It took him a while to speak. "Wow. Awesome, kid. It's very rare," he said finally. "Do you really have one? Did you read it?" He was breathing hard. Definitely excited.

"Yeah. It was pretty awesome," I said.

He stared hard at me. His eyes glowed. His narrow shoulders twitched under the oil company shirt. I realized the shirt was much too big for him.

"Sonny, want to sell it to me?" he asked.

"My name is Marco," I said.

"Want to sell it? I'll give you a good price. Really." His expression was intense. Like his life depended on getting that book.

Drops of sweat popped up on his forehead. He didn't even try to hide how excited he was.

"I . . . don't . . . think so," I said.

"Seriously. I'll give you a really good price," Sammy said. He wiped sweat out of his eyes with the back of his hand.

I thought about the superpower chapters in the back of the book. I hadn't tried them all. Sure, it was crazy. But my two tries had almost worked.

What if I had a superpower of some kind and didn't know it?

"I really don't want to sell," I told Sammy. "I need it for my collection. I have them all, see."

"I'll buy your collection!" Sammy said. "Tell me. How much do you want for the whole collection?"

I took a step back. He was so crazed, he was spitting when he talked.

"Sorry," I said. "I want to keep my collection."

"What if I give you a hundred dollars for *The Wizard of Ooze*?" Sammy asked. "What if I give you *three* hundred dollars?"

I stared up at him. "For just that one book?"

He nodded. He wiped more sweat off his red forehead.

"That's a lot of money," I said.

He brought his face close to mine. "So you'll do it?"

"No," I said. "Sorry. I really want to keep it. I—"

"OK, OK," Sammy said. He took a deep breath. "No problem. No worries. Here. Take this, sonny." He handed me a little white card. He pulled a stub of a pencil from his shirt pocket.

"What is this?" I asked.

"Fill it out," he said. He handed me the pencil. "Just put down your name and address. To get on the Ooze mailing list. You'll get all kinds of terrific offers."

I leaned the card against the wall and filled it out. I started to hand it back to Sammy. But a shadow fell over him. A figure stepped up behind him.

I uttered a gasp – and dropped the card.

And I stared into the black, oily face of The Ooze!

12

He was *immense*!

I mean, Sammy was tall. A lot taller than me. But The Ooze stood over him like a *mountain*!

His head was lumpy, bubbly with the shine of oil. His eyes were black and round. When he opened his mouth, I saw two jagged rows of teeth around a *bright blue tongue*!

His broad shoulders oozed out from under the straps of the black overalls that were his costume. His muscles rippled, wet, gleaming.

He even *smelled* like oil!

I stumbled back. My mouth dropped open. "Are you for real?" The words tumbled out.

"Yeah. Sure, kid," he rasped. "And SpongeBob SquarePants is running for president!"

Sammy giggled.

"Know what I mean?" The Ooze said, talking out of the side of his mouth. His famous slogan.

Sammy giggled again. He edged away from

The Ooze. His eyes were on me.

"That's an awesome costume!" I exclaimed.

"I like *your* costume, too," The Ooze shot back. "What are you dressed as – a total geek?"

I laughed. This guy was as mean as the *real* Ooze! He was a really good actor.

"Can you sign a book for me?" I asked him.

He growled at me. "Get lost, kid. I'm on my break."

Black gunk dripped like thick tar down his arms. His bumpy head was covered in goo. He clenched and unclenched his wet fists.

"Hey, boss, Marco here says he has the original issue," Sammy told him.

The Ooze guy froze in place. "No kidding." He gazed down at me. "What's a punk like you doing with that book? It's a very rare edition."

"I – I know," I stammered.

The Ooze guy turned to Sammy. "I'd love to get my hands on that book."

Sammy picked up the card I'd filled out and studied it. "Me, too," he said. "Listen, Marco – if you change your mind, I'll pay you three hundred dollars for that book. Think about it."

I knew I didn't want to sell. But I said, "OK. Maybe."

I said goodbye and started to walk away. I'd forgotten all about Gabriella. I saw her waving to me from the Weasel World booth down the aisle.

"You won't believe what just happened to me," I said.

"Tell me on the bus," she said. "I'm late. I promised my mom I'd get home in time to walk the dog."

She started to pull me towards the exit. "Whoa. Wait." I felt a blast of heat on my back. A shadow swept over me. I inhaled a sharp, sour odour.

I spun around. The guy in the Ooze costume stood right behind us.

"Hey, kiddo," he rasped, leaning close.

"Wow," I muttered. "How do you get your costume to give off heat like that? It's like standing in front of an oven!"

"Too hot for you, kid?" he rumbled. "Then listen to me. I really think you should change your mind about selling that book."

Gabriella and I exchanged glances.

The Ooze guy gazed around the convention hall. "You won't always be in a big crowd," he muttered. "And I have lots of ways to persuade you. *Know what I mean?*"

"Oh, wow." My legs started to tremble. I felt a chill of fear run down my whole body.

Was he threatening me?

13

"That guy in the big black costume tried to scare me," I told Gabriella. We were sitting near the front of the crowded bus. People jammed the aisle. A man standing over me kept poking me with his umbrella.

"I heard him. He was just doing his job," Gabriella said. "He was supposed to act tough to everybody. You know. Put on a show."

"But he stood so close, I smell like tar!" I cried.

Gabriella laughed. "Actually, he was pretty funny."

The man's umbrella jabbed my knee. The bus stopped, and more people crushed into the aisle. Rain pattered the window behind Gabriella and me.

"I think the Ooze guy was serious," I said. "He and that guy Sammy who works for him really wanted my book."

"Did they say they'd buy it from you?" Gabriella asked.

I nodded. "Sammy said he'd pay three hundred dollars."

Gabriella blew out a whoosh of air. "Wow, Marco. That's a *ton* of money. You could buy that new game system you want!"

"I know," I said, "but—"

"Three hundred dollars for a comic book you got for free!"

"I know," I repeated. "But . . . maybe I want to keep it for my collection."

And maybe I wanted to keep it to try more superpower experiments.

I didn't say that to Gabriella.

The bus jerked to a halt. People staggered and stumbled. The aisle cleared a little as people climbed off.

And I saw something at the back of the bus that made me gasp.

I grabbed Gabriella's sleeve. "Look." I pointed to the back seat.

"What's your problem?" Gabriella said. Then she saw him, too.

The guy in the Ooze costume.

He was spread out over the entire back of the bus. There was room for four or five people across the back. But he took up the whole row!

I felt a stab of panic in my chest. "He's following us!" I cried.

Gabriella bit her bottom lip. "Maybe."

"We'll know if he gets off when we do," I said. "He's going to follow me to my house – isn't he? He's going to force me to give him the book."

"He – he can't do that!" Gabriella stammered. She was trying to sound brave. But I could tell she was as frightened as I was.

"Look. He's staring hard at us," I said. "Sending us a message."

Gabriella stared back at him. "Maybe he finished work at the convention and he's taking the bus home," she said.

I shook my head. "He's following us. I know he is. Look at the way he's staring at us. Not blinking or anything. With that ugly scowl on his face."

I jumped to my feet. "Let's get off here."

"But this isn't our stop!" Gabriella said.

"We can walk from here," I said. "It's only a few more blocks." I glanced to the back. The Ooze guy hadn't moved.

The bus squealed as it stopped. The door slid open. I squeezed past a large woman with two shopping bags and leaped out the front door.

Rain pattered my head. My shoes slid on the wet pavement.

I turned and saw Gabriella jump off the bus. We both jogged away from the bus stop.

The bus doors closed. The bus pulled away from the kerb.

"No Ooze," I said. I let out a sigh of relief. "He didn't get off with us."

But as the bus rumbled away, I saw him in the back window. His sludgy face was pressed against the glass. And he was staring hard at us. His eyes locked on us until the bus moved out of view.

"Weird," Gabriella muttered. "He definitely was trying to frighten you."

I nodded. "Well, he's pretty scary," I said. I wiped raindrops off my face. "I wonder what he looks like when he takes off the mask and the costume."

"Forget about him," Gabriella said. And then she added in a low growl, *"Know what I mean?"*

We jogged to our houses, ducking our heads against the rain. By the time I got home, I was *soaked.*

Mum and Dad were in the kitchen. They were both at the counter, chopping up vegetables for a salad.

"How was the comic convention?" Mum asked.

"Nice," I said.

She gazed up from her carrots. "You didn't buy anything?"

"No. Just looked," I said.

"You're drenched," Dad said. "And what's that smell? You smell like tar!"

"I . . . guess I stood too close to The Ooze," I replied.

"Go upstairs and get changed," Mum said. "Your dad and I are going out in a bit. I'll need you to watch Zeke."

"No problem," I replied. I hurried up the stairs.

I can do some superpower tests now, I decided.

I still had a lot of chapters to go. I had come close the first two times. Maybe I could discover a special power inside myself.

I stepped into my room. I pulled the wet T-shirt off and tossed it into a corner.

Then I hurried over to my bed to pick up the book where I'd left it.

Not there.

"Hmmmm." I pulled back the covers. Not there. But I knew that's where I'd left it. Face down at the bottom of the bed.

I checked my desk. My dresser. Looked on the floor beneath my bed. Searched my bookshelves.

I opened the wardrobe and frantically pulled up the piles of dirty clothes I'd tossed on the floor. No. Not there.

Not anywhere.

My head spun. My heart pounded.

The book was GONE.

14

I dropped down on to the edge of my bed and took a deep breath. I shut my eyes and tried to remember. . .

Did I hide the book somewhere before I left for the comic convention? Did I put it away?

No. I had left it open on the bed. I remembered clearly.

I opened my eyes – and heard a voice nearby. A cough. A soft chuckle.

I walked to the bedroom door and peered into my brother's room. There was Zeke, sitting cross-legged on the floor with the graphic novel in his lap.

"Hey!" I shouted. I stomped into his room.

He made a startled yelp. He raised his eyes for a second. Then lowered his head back to the book.

"Keep your mitts off my stuff!" I shouted. I swiped the book out of his hands. "You're too young for this!"

"Wanna bet?" Zeke cried. He made a wild grab for the book.

I swung it away from him.

Zeke jumped to his feet. "I have superhero strength!" he exclaimed. He threw himself at me, wrapped his arms around my waist – and tried to wrestle me to the floor.

"Let go! Let go of me!" I shouted.

He made another grab for the book. I swung it behind my back.

He pushed me down to the floor and climbed on top of my chest. "Superhero strength!" he shouted.

"Wimp strength," I said.

He gave me a hard punch in the ribs. "Give it back to me, Marco. Give it!"

"Stop it!" I screamed. "Get off me, you punk!"

I turned and saw Mum in the doorway. She shook her head angrily at me.

"Marco, stop it! No fighting with your little brother!" she snapped.

I gasped. "Huh? Me?"

"And stop calling him names," Mum said.

Zeke climbed off my chest and put on his pouty face. "He hurt me, Mummy!" he cried. He ran over to her and hugged her waist. "He really hurt me."

Total phony.

"I mean it, Marco," Mum said. "I've had enough."

"But – but – but – " I sputtered.

"You're grounded," Mum said. "Now go make yourself useful. Go down to the laundry room. Take all the wet clothes from the washer and put them in the dryer. When they're dry, I want you to fold them all neatly and put them away."

"But Mum – that's not fair," I said. "That's *work*!"

"Do a good job and maybe you won't be grounded for too long," Mum said.

"Yeah. Do a good job," Zeke repeated. He stuck his tongue out at me.

Mum went back downstairs. I muttered some bad words under my breath. But I didn't say anything to Zeke. I didn't want him to get me in any more trouble.

Maybe he thought I'd forget about the book and leave it in his room. But I carried it to my room and closed the door behind me. I hid it under the pile of dirty clothes in my wardrobe.

Then I went down to the laundry room and pulled the wet clothes into the dryer. I hate wet clothes. They just feel so yucky.

But I did the job as fast as I could because I was eager to get back to my room. Back to the Ooze book.

A few minutes later, I had my door closed tight and the book spread out in front of me on the bed. I turned to the chapters at the back, and I began to read...

Perhaps you are a water hero. It's easy to find out. Fill your bathtub to the top with ice cubes and cold water. Then...

15

"I'm f-f-freezing!" I stuttered.

I was in the tub, up to my neck in icy water. My skin was red and tingly. Ice cubes bobbed and bumped against me.

First I had the shivers. Then I had the DEEP shivers.

"Th-this is crazy," I moaned. My teeth started to chatter. "It's n-not working."

Oh, wait.

Yes, it *was*!

The shaking and shivering and chattering suddenly stopped. Was it just because my whole body was totally *numb*?

No. I felt different. I felt my body changing.

I'm melting! I thought. I suddenly felt weak . . . soft . . . so light.

I'm dissolving. I'm melting . . . changing into WATER!

No skin. No bones. Just water.

And then the weakness lifted. And I felt a surge of power. Like a bolt of electricity shooting through me.

And I rose up in the bathtub. Like a wave. Like a mighty tidal wave. An amazing feeling!

It lasted about ten seconds.

I stretched high ... higher ... then splashed back down. And the cold water seeped over my shoulders. The ice cubes bobbed against my waist.

I felt cold again. I felt FROZEN again! And I started to shake and shiver.

I was trembling so hard, I could barely grip the sides of the tub. I tried to pull myself out. But my legs were frozen numb.

"*Uh-uh-uh-uh-uh.*" A crazy sound kept repeating through my chattering teeth. "*Uh-uh-uh-uh.*"

Finally, I lifted myself out of the tub. I couldn't stand. I rolled on to the floor. I lay there on my back, shaking and groaning. I smacked my frozen hands together like a seal. I kicked my feet in the air.

Numb. Everything was frozen numb. My hands and feet tingled with cold pain.

Somehow I grabbed a bath towel off the towel rack. I struggled to wrap it around me.

"I'll n-never be warm," I murmured. "N-never b-be warm again!"

I wrapped another towel around me. Then I half stumbled, half crawled to my room.

I pulled on three shirts, two sweaters and my warmest sweatpants. I climbed under the covers.

But I couldn't stop the chills from running down my back. Couldn't stop my body from trembling like I was in a powerful earthquake.

I have to find out what I'm doing wrong, I decided. *Why do the powers last only ten seconds?*

If I ever warm up enough so I can walk again, I have to go back to the comic convention. I have to talk to that guy Sammy. He seemed all right. Not like The Ooze. Maybe he can tell me what I'm doing wrong.

I buried my frozen face in the pillow. Under the covers, I pulled myself into a tight ball. If only I could stop shaking and quaking!

I glanced at the clock on my bed table. Four-thirty. Still early. Time enough to take the Ooze book to Sammy at the convention and see if he had any advice.

A few minutes later, I started to feel more normal. My skin was still red and blotchy. But I had some feeling back in my hands and feet. I took off the two sweaters and two of the shirts. I changed into jeans. And I pulled on my trainers.

I grabbed the book and hurried downstairs. I found Mum in the den. "Mum, I have to go back to the comic convention," I said. "I forgot to do something there."

Mum looked up from the magazine she was reading. "Sorry, Marco. You're grounded, remember?"

"But Mum," I pleaded. "It's very important. Maybe you could *un*ground me – just for the rest of the afternoon."

She shook her head. "No. Did you finish the laundry?"

"Almost," I said.

Should I tell her the truth? That I need advice about getting superpowers?

No. No way anyone would believe that.

"Mum, a guy at the convention wants to give me three hundred dollars for this Ooze book." I held it up. I was telling the truth. I just didn't tell her that I had no plans to sell it.

She lowered the magazine to her lap. "That's a lot of money, Marco. Are you sure this man is honest?"

"Yes," I said. "Does that mean I can go?"

"No," Mum replied. "Remember? I told you that Dad and I have to go out. I need you to stay home and watch Zeke."

"But Mum—"

She gave me that hard stare with her forehead

wrinkled and her eyebrows pointing down to her nose. I knew that stare very well. It meant, *Shut up, Marco, if you know what's good for you.*

So I shut up.

I made an unhappy face. I muttered a few more words under my breath. Then I tucked the book under my arm and slunk back upstairs to my room.

A little while later, Mum and Dad said goodbye. And to take good care of Zeke.

I heard the car back down the drive. Mum gave two short honks before she reached the street. It's something she always does. I'm not sure why. Then she drove off with Dad.

As soon as she was gone, Zeke came skipping into my room. "What do you want to do, Marco?" he asked. "Want to play a game?"

I stared at him. And then I stared at the Ooze book.

And suddenly, I knew what I wanted to do.

I knew what I *had* to do.

16

"Put on your shoes," I said. "We're going to the comic convention."

His mouth dropped open. "Huh?"

"You said you wanted to go," I told him. "Well, here's your chance."

Zeke grinned. "Cool!" He started for his room. Then he stopped. "But Mum said—"

"You can't tell Mum," I said. "It's a secret. Can you keep a secret?"

He crossed his heart with two fingers. "I promise." He ran up the stairs two at a time.

I knew he couldn't be trusted. Zeke is a little snitch. But what choice did I have?

My mission was clear. I had to rush to the convention before it closed. Show the book to Sammy. See what he had to say. And get back home with Zeke before Mum and Dad returned.

Tense. Very tense. But it could be done.

I pulled on my jacket. I tucked the book under my arm. "Zeke?" I shouted up the stairs. "Where are you? What's taking so long?"

"Can't find one of my shoes," he called.

I groaned. *I should just leave him here,* I thought.

But I couldn't. Mum had put me in charge. If I left him alone, Zeke would get in some kind of big trouble – just to make me look bad.

I ran up to his room. He was pounding his fist into his pillow. *Pound pound pound.* That's what he always does when he can't find something. He's such a jerk.

I found the other trainer under the bed in two seconds. Then I tossed him his jacket, got him downstairs and pushed him out the front door.

It was a windy, cool evening. The rain had stopped, but the sky was still dark with clouds.

"Run," I said. "We're going to be too late."

We ran to the bus stop on the next corner. No bus in sight. I began to pace back and forth with the book tucked under my arm.

Zeke leaned against an old tree and started to pick at the bark. He pulled off a big chunk and tossed it to the grass.

"Why are you doing that?" I asked.

He shrugged. "For fun?"

More time passed. Finally, I saw the bus turn

a corner and head our way. A few seconds later, we climbed on and took seats near the back.

I stared out the dusty window, watching the sun dip low behind the clouds. *We're not going to make it*, I thought. *Unless the bus really rockets.*

But the bus didn't rocket. We kept stopping every few blocks to let people on. And then as we got close to downtown, there was some kind of accident up ahead.

I stared out at the flashing red lights. We didn't move at all.

Zeke poked me hard with his elbow. "Let me hold the book."

"Why?" I said.

"Because I want to," he said. He poked me again. "Let me hold the book. Or I'll tell Mum and Dad you took me to the convention."

What a punk.

"OK. Here." I shoved the book on to his lap.

He didn't open it or anything. Just held it.

The bus finally started to move again. We crawled past the flashing police lights. But I couldn't see the accident.

About ten minutes later, we were downtown. I pulled Zeke off the bus. It was really late. I could see a pale white moon between the clouds.

The pavements were jammed with people coming in our direction. I knew what that meant.

They were all coming out of the convention centre. Because the comic convention was over.

. Closed.

I let out a long sigh.

"Check it out!" Zeke cried. He pointed to two girls in Werewolf Woman costumes. "Cool!"

I was too disappointed to speak.

Zeke stopped to admire a big poster of The Mutant Crocodile Rangers. "Awesome!" he cried.

At least *one* of us was happy.

People rushed past us, carrying comics and posters.

I studied every face. Maybe I would see Sammy. Maybe I'd get lucky and catch him on his way out.

Some kids pushed past me, singing the Dr Weird-Face anthem at the top of their lungs. One of them had a Dr Weird-Face bobblehead doll that he kept shaking up and down.

We were nearly to the front entrance of the convention centre. No sign of Sammy. Guards were locking the big glass front doors.

I walked along the side of the building. The sky turned even darker.

No, wait. It wasn't the sky. It was a shadow. A deep shadow rolled over me as if a cloud had passed over my head.

And the guy in the Ooze costume rose up to

block my path.

I gasped in surprise. I backed against the cold concrete wall.

The guy pressed up close. And once again, I could smell the tar off his skin. His cheeks appeared to bubble on his face. When he opened his mouth, his blue tongue darted from side to side.

He stuck a huge wet hand out. "The book, kid," he growled. His voice came from deep in his chest. "Hand it over. Now."

I swallowed hard. My chest suddenly felt fluttery.

He had me backed against the wall. I couldn't move.

Without warning, he reached down and raised his hand over my head. He squeezed his fist – and I felt something drip on to my head.

"Owwww!" I cried out. It was burning hot!

He squeezed his fist again. And sent another drip of burning oil on to my hair. It burned my scalp. I could feel it dripping down to my ears.

I screamed again. "Stop it!" My voice came out high and shrill.

My brain whirred.

How is he doing that? Is he just a guy in a costume?

Or is he the real Ooze? A real-life villain?

He waved his oily fist in front of my face again.

"The book, kid. I'm not playing games."

"OK, OK," I said. My voice cracked. "I'll give it to you. But that guy Sammy promised me three hundred dollars for it."

He shook his head. "Sammy changed his mind," he growled. *"Know what I mean?"*

"But – but — " I sputtered. "Will you pay me for it?"

"No. You're giving it to me. I guess your brain needs a little more time to *warm up* to the idea!"

He raised his fist over my head. He squeezed it hard.

I screamed again as the hot oil scorched my scalp.

"No, please... " I tried to cover my head with my hands. "You win. I'll give it to you."

He lowered his fist. He leaned over me, his black eyes burning into mine. His blue tongue darted rapidly in and out of his mouth.

"My little brother has it," I said. "Zeke, give him the book."

I spun around. "Zeke? Hey – Zeke?"

Oh, no. Oh, no.

He was *gone*.

17

"Zeke! Hey – Zeke!"

I began to shout as loudly as I could.

"Zeke! Where are you? Come here! Zeke?"

I leaned past the hulking body of The Ooze. No sign of Zeke behind him.

I spun all around and shouted my little brother's name over and over till my voice cracked.

"Nice try, kid," The Ooze rasped. "Why don't you just admit that you *don't have* a little brother?"

"But – but I do!" I sputtered.

He stared down at me, cold as a glacier. "Where is the book?" he boomed. "At home? Is it at your house? Do you want to go get it for me?"

"N-no," I stammered. "My little brother has it. He's here. Really."

I cupped my hands around my mouth and shouted Zeke's name some more.

No sign of him.

The convention centre had emptied out. Only a few people were gathered in small groups in front of the building.

The Ooze leaned over me. "The little-brother trick isn't going to work," he growled. *"Know what I mean?"*

"Y-yes, I know what you're saying," I choked out. "But Zeke —"

He pushed my chest, backing me up against the wall. "I really want that book," he snarled. He wiped black sticky stuff on the front of my jacket. "You seem like a smart kid."

"Thanks," I muttered.

"Too bad I have to *ooze* you!" he boomed.

"Ooze me?" I cried.

I knew what it meant. In his comic stories, he oozed people on nearly every page. I always enjoyed it. I actually thought it was *funny*!

I had no idea it could ever happen to me in *real life*.

"You're really The Ooze – aren't you?" I cried. "You're not a man in a costume. You're real. You're alive!"

"Don't ask questions, Marco," he said. "You don't want to know the answer."

"Yes, I do," I insisted. "I . . ."

"You're stalling," he said. "You're scared.

You're shaking. You know you're about to be oozed."

My heart pounded so hard, I could barely breathe. I made one last, frantic search for Zeke.

No sign of him.

I knew what it meant to be oozed. It meant that first he would cover me in burning hot oil. Then he was going to dive on top of me. He was going to crush me under him – *bury* me under a huge, heavy tidal wave of oily hot sludge.

Trembling, I gazed up at him. "Please . . . "

His whole body started to bubble. He shook. He shimmered.

He rose up tall . . . taller . . . and heaved himself closer.

I could feel the heat against my face. My skin started to burn.

His shadow swept over me. The whole world grew darker than night.

He raised both fists over my head, ready to squeeze the sizzling oil on me.

"Hey, kid," he boomed, "any last words?"

18

I shut my eyes. My muscles all clamped tight. I gritted my teeth so hard, my jaw hurt.

I could feel the heat press over me. Smell the tar. Hear the bubbling of his oily skin.

"Goodbye, kid." His voice rumbled over me like thunder.

And then I heard another voice. A boy's voice: "Can I have your autograph?"

It sounded far away, like from the other side of a wall.

"Please?" the voice said. "Could you sign this for me?"

And then another voice. A girl's voice: "Can we have our picture taken with you?"

I opened my eyes. I could still see only black. The heat off The Ooze's bubbling skin scorched my face.

"I'm your biggest fan," the boy said.

"Can I have your autograph, too?" another boy

chimed in.

The Ooze turned away from me.

The air suddenly felt cooler. I blinked several times, waiting for my eyes to see again.

He spun away to greet his fans. Five or six kids stood in a tight group, waving autograph books up at him. One girl had her phone raised to take his picture.

I waited until the kids surrounded The Ooze. Then I took a deep breath – and pushed myself away from the wall.

My legs felt unsteady and weak. My head spun. I nearly toppled face first to the ground.

Somehow, I caught my balance. I lowered my head – and ran.

"Hey!" I heard The Ooze roar.

But I didn't turn back. My legs felt a little stronger with each step. My head began to clear as the sickening odour faded.

I turned the corner and kept running. My shoes slapped the pavement. My hands swung wildly at my sides as I ran.

I saw a group of teenagers staring at me. "Whoa! Look at his hair!" someone shouted.

I must have looked crazy, running like a wild man with my hair covered in thick black oil. But I didn't slow down.

I didn't slow down until a boy tackled me around the waist.

We both fell hard to the pavement. I let out a cry as I cracked my elbow and pain shot through my body.

I rolled over. Scrambled to my knees. And stared at the boy. He wore an ugly purple monster mask, so I couldn't see his face.

"Who are you?" I cried. "What do you want?"

19

The boy's brown eyes stared out at me through the eye slits of the mask. "Marco, it's *me*!" he cried.

"Zeke?"

He nodded. He jumped to his feet and helped pull me up.

"Where were you?" I demanded.

"I bought this mask," he said. "I want to be a supervillain."

"You ARE a supervillain!" I shouted. "I was almost OOZED because of you!"

He laughed. I don't know why he thought that was funny. He's such a total weirdo.

"It's not funny!" I cried. I tried to shove him, but he danced away.

I saw the Ooze book on the pavement. Zeke must have dropped it when he tackled me.

I grabbed it. I gazed all around. No sign of The Ooze. Was he still signing autographs?

"We – we have to get out of here," I stammered.

I hugged the book tightly to my chest and started to run towards the bus stop. I turned. Zeke was still standing there, fiddling with the rubber mask.

"Hurry!" I shouted, waving hard. "This is no joke!"

"*Grrrrr.*" He growled and clawed his hands at me like a tiger.

"Come on – run!" I begged.

He didn't move. "You just want to get home before Mum and Dad so you don't get in trouble."

I knew I had no time to argue with him. I ran back and grabbed his hand. I gave him a hard tug. "Let's go."

We ran about half a block. Then we both froze when we saw a man running towards us.

The man was *on fire*!

Bright orange flames shot off his body. He wore dark trousers and a dark turtleneck sweater. Flames flicked and darted off his clothes, off his head, his feet.

But he didn't scream. He came trotting towards us steadily.

I uttered a gasp when I realized his clothing didn't burn. His whole body was covered in darting flames – but he didn't burn at all!

I staggered back. I tried to get out of his way.

"Do you need help?" I screamed. "Can we help you?"

Flames flickered off him and died on the pavement. He didn't make a sound as he ran steadily towards us.

Zeke and I both leaped into the street, trying to avoid him.

But we were too shocked and confused to move fast. He roared up to us, flames flying.

"What do you *want*?" I screamed.

His hand shot out.

"OW!" I felt the heat of the flames.

He grabbed the book with a flaming hand. Jerked it hard from my grasp. Then he spun away – and with flames dancing and crackling all around him, ran back the way he'd come.

20

People screamed and pointed at the man as he ran down the street.

Zeke and I didn't move. I guess we were in shock. I could still feel the heat of the fire on my skin and clothes.

I realized I was trembling. Zeke pulled the monster mask off his face. His eyes were wide with fright. He grabbed my hand.

"Who was that man?" he asked in a tiny voice.

I shook my head. "Beats me."

"He – he took your book," Zeke stammered. "He was . . . on fire, Marco. He was really on fire."

"I know," I said softly. I let out a long sigh. "Let's go home."

We beat Mum and Dad home by about ten minutes.

I made Zeke swear again that he wouldn't tell

them what we'd done. He nodded quietly. "They wouldn't believe us anyway," he said. "I mean, about the man on fire."

He was right. I wasn't sure I believed it, either.

Actually, I desperately wanted to tell my parents about The Ooze, and the flaming man, and how my book was stolen. But Zeke was right. They wouldn't believe it. And it would only get me into major trouble.

Mum and Dad walked into the house, carrying big bags of groceries. The first thing Mum asked was, "Did you two get along OK? No fights?"

"Yeah, fine," I answered. "No fights."

"What did you two do?" Dad asked.

"Stuff," I said.

At dinner, Zeke and I both tried to act normal. It wasn't easy.

And it wasn't easy for me to get to sleep that night.

I kept seeing The Ooze rising up and preparing to pour hot oil over me. Again and again, I heard his growl: *Hey, kid, any last words?*

And then the burning man. Staring at Zeke and me through the flames. Grabbing the book and running off without saying a word.

Why was the book so important? So valuable?

Everyone knows the origin of The Ooze.

The first part of the book couldn't be important to anyone.

So it had to be the chapters in the back that interested these guys. The chapters about finding your superpower.

But those chapters didn't work. Well, they only worked for ten seconds.

So why were people so eager to get their hands on that book?

I finally fell asleep with the question rolling around and around in my brain.

I fell into a restless sleep – and had a frightening nightmare.

The dream started with a view of my bedroom window. The window was open wide. The curtains were fluttering in a stiff wind.

The curtains made a slapping sound as they flew back against the wall. The wind howled. It sounded like an animal crying.

In the dream, I felt frightened. Why was the window open? I always sleep with it tightly shut.

Slap . . . slap . . . slap. . .

The curtains slapped hard against the wall. Then, in the dream, they slowly changed shape. They formed arms and legs. The curtains became ghosts, howling ghosts.

Slap . . . slap . . . slap. . .

I woke up with a gasp. I was drenched in

sweat. My pyjamas stuck to my skin.

The air in my room was burning hot. Suffocating.

I glimpsed pale light pouring through the bedroom window. To my shock, it *was* wide open. Just as in the dream.

And then I felt a drip on my forehead. Burning-hot liquid.

With a trembling hand, I clicked on my bed-table lamp.

And gazed up at The Ooze. His dark eyes stared angrily down at me. He had his fist raised. He squeezed another drop of scalding hot oil on to my forehead.

I pressed my hand against the burning skin. "Please..." I uttered.

"The book," he growled. "Give it to me."

The disgusting smell, the boiling heat rolling off his body in waves...

I couldn't breathe. I couldn't move.

He was in my house! In my *room*! Leaning over my bed with his oily fist raised.

"I – I—" I struggled to speak.

"The book, kid," he growled. "I'm not playing games here. *Know what I mean?*"

"But—"

He swept his arm slowly and dripped a streak of oil down my bedspread. It made a sizzling sound. The bedspread smoked and split apart.

"That could be you, punk," The Ooze growled. "You ever hear human skin sizzle like that? It isn't pretty."

"But I don't have the book!" I finally managed to choke out.

His whole head appeared to bubble. The oily muscles on his shoulders rippled. His blue tongue whipped from side to side.

"No games, Marco," he rasped. "No games and no lies."

"It was st-stolen!" I stammered. I was sitting straight up in bed, hugging my knees to keep from shaking.

"Liar!" The Ooze boomed. He splashed hot oil across the bed. The bedspread smoked and sizzled again.

"I'm telling the truth!" I cried.

He leaned closer. The heavy sour smell was so strong, I started to gag.

"Get the book, Marco. Don't make me ooze you. Why mess up such a nice room?"

"The book was stolen," I insisted. "I'm telling the truth. Someone stole it from me this afternoon."

His skin bubbled harder. His dark eyes appeared to sink deep into his wet, oily face.

He shook his head slowly. "Oh, Marco," he said softly. "Oh, Marco. Oh, Marco. I'm going to make you *so sorry* you said that."

21

"MUM! DAD! Help me!"

The hoarse scream burst from my throat.

My cry seemed to startle The Ooze. His black eyes went wide. He staggered back a step.

"MUM! DAD!" I shrieked. "I need HELP! *Hurry!*"

The Ooze jabbed his open hand in my face. "Shut up, punk. Just give me the book. Give it to me and I'll beat it."

"MUM! DAD! Hurry!" I screamed.

Over the pounding of my heart, I heard footsteps. Fast footsteps coming down the hall.

The Ooze heard them, too. To my surprise, he spun away from me.

"I don't need this," he growled. *"Know what I mean?"*

He lumbered to the open window. He grabbed the window frame and hoisted his huge body on to the ledge.

"I'll be back," he growled. And then he let go of the window and jumped out. Vanished into the night.

I was still huddled in my bed, shaking and shivering. The sickening tar odour lingered in my nose. I could still feel the disgusting wet heat from The Ooze's body.

The door shot open. Mum and Dad tore into the room, wrapping their bathrobes around them. Wide-eyed and alarmed.

"Marco? What happened?"

"Marco? What's wrong?"

Their eyes went to the floor. They both gasped in surprise and confusion.

I followed their gaze. And saw the big oily black footprints on my white bedroom rug.

"What's that?" Dad cried. "Who did that?"

And then Mum saw the burns in the bedspread. The ragged splits in the material.

"Marco – you've got some explaining to do! What have you done to your room? Have you gone CRAZY?"

"It's . . . my science experiment," I said. "It's not working."

"What kind of science experiment?" Mum cried. "An experiment to ruin your room?"

"I'm sorry. I'll clean it all up in the morning. I promise."

"You'll do more than clean it up," Dad said. He stared at the black footprints and shook his head. "I want a full explanation of this science experiment in the morning."

"It's for extra credit," I said. That usually wins them over. But I knew it wouldn't work this time.

Mum yawned loudly. "I've got to get some sleep. We'll talk about this in the morning, OK?"

"OK," I said.

Dad studied me for a long moment. Then he followed Mum out of the room.

The oily black footprints glowed in the light from my lamp.

I had to tell someone about this. I couldn't keep it to myself.

I couldn't tell Mum and Dad. They wouldn't understand. And I couldn't tell Zeke. He was too little. And too weird. It would probably just make him laugh.

"Gabriella." I murmured her name. "Yes. Gabriella."

I glanced at the bed-table clock. Two in the morning.

I knew I couldn't call her this late. Her parents would kill both of us!

I grabbed my mobile phone with a trembling hand. I clicked open the keyboard and texted her. I typed text after text.

I told her everything, starting with my dream. I told her about the open window . . . the oily footprints . . . how The Ooze wanted to ooze me earlier . . . how the book was stolen.

My thumbs flew. I typed and typed. It felt good to get the story out. To tell someone I could trust. I knew Gabriella would believe me. And I knew she wouldn't tell anyone else.

I sent the texts. Then I sat on the edge of my bed, staring at the phone.

No reply. Of course not. It was the middle of the night. Gabriella had to be sound asleep.

"She'll see it first thing in the morning," I told myself.

I climbed back under the covers. I wanted to go back to sleep.

But how could I? That big, dangerous creep had broken into my room. And I knew he would come back.

"I have to destroy him before he destroys me!"

The words escaped my lips. I knew I sounded like a character in a comic book.

A comic book. . .

My mind spun. I pictured all the Ooze books I had read. And suddenly . . . I knew how I could destroy him.

"Oh!"

I let out a cry when I heard scraping sounds at my window.

I realized I'd forgotten to close it. I'd left it wide open.

The Ooze! The Ooze was back already!

I jerked straight up and stared in horror.

Stared at a flash of blinding yellow light.

And a scream of shock and horror burst from my throat.

22

The flaming man filled the window with his fiery light.

Bright sparks shot off his head and body. He rolled through the window, on to my bedroom floor – a blazing fireball.

"No!" I cried. I jumped out of bed.

The Ooze had left oil all over my rug. Would this guy's flames start a huge fire?

I started to run to the door. But my blanket tangled around my ankles, and I fell face down in front of him.

The flames crackled as they darted out from his dark clothing. He raised both arms, and flames shot straight up, nearly touching the ceiling.

He glared at me with his green eyes. The rest of his face was hidden behind the bright curtain of red and yellow.

"Where is it?" His voice rushed at me like the

roar of a bonfire.

I blinked. I didn't know how to answer.

"Where is it?" he repeated. *"Where did you hide it?"*

"Huh?"

I pulled my legs free from the blanket. I stumbled back against the bed.

The flames shooting off his body made wild shadows jump and dance. Sparks landed on my desk, my dresser, and fizzled out.

"You – you already took it!" I finally found my voice. "What do you want? You already have it!"

"NOOOOO!" A burst of fire shot out all around him. *"Where did you hide it?"*

"I – I – I –" I stuttered. "I don't understand! What are you *talking* about? You *have* the book!"

Moving quickly, he began circling my room. His fiery hands swept the papers off my desk. He pulled open dresser drawers.

Flames scorched the wallpaper. Smoky embers crackled on the carpet.

"Where issssss it?" he hissed.

"You – you're going to set my room on fire!" I cried.

"I'll burn it all down if you don't hand it over to me!" he shouted. He raised his hand to the curtains. *"Watch it all burn."*

"No. Please – I don't understand."

I edged my way to my wardrobe. I suddenly remembered something. On the wardrobe floor near the back.

If only I could get there in time. . .

"I – I'm getting it for you," I stammered.

I had no idea what he wanted. He had the Ooze book. What more could I give him?

But I had to stall him. I had to get to the wardrobe. I knew it was my only chance.

He stepped away from the curtains to watch me. The flames from his hands retreated.

"I'm getting it," I repeated. "It's in here."

I pulled open the wardrobe door and stepped inside. I had to duck low under my hanging clothes.

I couldn't see anything. It was pitch-black inside the wardrobe.

I bent down and fumbled through the stuff on the floor. Feeling blindly, I pushed shoes and trainers out of the way.

"Where issss it?" the flaming man called. I could hear the flames hiss with each word.

"Found it!" I cried.

I gripped the little metal fire extinguisher and pulled it off the wardrobe floor. My dad put a fire extinguisher in every room. Of course, I never thought I would have to use it.

In the darkness, I turned the canister. Found the trigger. Steadied it in my hand. Ready to shoot. Ready to blast him.

"Found it!" I shouted again.

"Hurry!" he boomed.

Stepping out of the wardrobe, I swung the fire extinguisher in front of me. Aimed the nozzle at his chest.

Squeezed the trigger.

Nothing happened.

23

He roared and jumped back, sending up a sheet of flames.

I shook the canister. Shook it so hard, I almost dropped it.

Then I lurched forwards. Dived across the room – and squeezed the trigger again with all my might.

A white spray shot out and hit the flames darting from his face.

"Hey!" He uttered a startled shout.

I kept the trigger down. I moved the spray up and down, from his face to his chest.

His flames flickered but didn't go out.

He stuck out his arms. He backed up to the window.

Breathing hard, my heart pounding, I moved forward. I kept the white spray on his face.

I could see the angry look in his eyes. He raised a hand to shield his eyes.

The canister made a sputtering sound. I struggled to keep the spray steady.

The flames didn't give up easily. They twisted and danced as if trying to squirm away from the spray.

The extinguisher felt lighter. I knew it was almost empty.

Suddenly, he turned away from me. He leaped to the window ledge – and then out. He flew out into the dark night. A bright fireball against the blackness.

I let out a long, shuddering sigh.

I couldn't stop trembling. The fire extinguisher fell from my hand and bounced on to the carpet.

I bent over and grabbed my knees. I struggled to catch my breath.

I sat down on the floor with my back against the bed. No way I could get back to sleep. I just sat there till morning, staring at the open window and thinking . . . thinking. . .

The next morning, Mom and Dad had to leave early. We didn't have our big discussion. Thank goodness!

The morning was cool and grey. It had rained during the night, and the pavement was dotted with deep puddles.

As I walked to school, I kept glancing behind me. I expected to see The Ooze or the fire guy pop out from behind a tree and come after me.

Every shadow made me jump. A dog barked nearby, and I nearly fell into a puddle!

By the time I made it to school, I was shaking.

I found Gabriella in front of her locker. She was talking to some girls from our class, so I had to wait.

The bell rang. Time to go into class. I followed after her.

"Gabriella, did you get my text messages?"

She nodded. Then she turned back and studied me. "Were they supposed to make sense?"

"Of course!" I cried. "What do you mean? You didn't believe me?"

She twisted up her face. "It wasn't a fiction story you wrote? For our Creative Writing project?"

"No," I said. "Why would I send you a story at two in the morning?"

"Marco, why do you do *anything*?" That made her laugh. She cracks herself up.

I didn't think it was funny. "It was all true," I said. "Last night—"

Mrs Hopper met us at the door. "Good morning, you two. Arguing again? Take your seats, OK?"

"We weren't arguing," Gabriella said. "We were just talking."

We don't sit together. Gabriella sits in the front row. I sit near the back.

"I have to talk to you," I said. "Meet me after school. OK?"

"Where?"

"You know where," I said. "Where we always meet. In the alley behind the Dairy Freeze."

"Do you have any money?" she asked. "Can you buy us cones?"

"My life is in *danger*!" I said. "I'm not really interested in ice cream!"

"Well, I am!" she replied, and trotted to her desk.

The alley behind the Dairy Freeze was lined with overflowing bins, old cartons, and other rubbish. Workers parked their cars back there. I could see store workers in their white aprons through the tiny back window.

Someone had left an old rusting bench on the other side of the alley. That's where I waited after school for Gabriella.

It was a good meeting place. No one ever came back here. You could buy an ice cream cone and sit on the bench. And the smell of the rubbish wasn't too bad at all.

I bought a chocolate cone with chocolate sprinkles and carried it back to the bench. I expected Gabriella to show up any second. But

I'd already finished the cone and was licking my fingers – and still no sign of her.

What's up with this? I thought. *I told her it was really important. Where is she?*

I checked the time on my mobile phone. Nearly four o'clock. School had been out for forty-five minutes.

I sighed. She wasn't going to show.

I watched two robins pecking around in the grass in the empty lot beside the store. Then I climbed to my feet, ready to leave.

I took a few steps around the side of the building towards the street. But I stopped when a wave of heat blasted against my face. I staggered back. I recognized the sharp, putrid smell. My skin prickled and burned.

The Ooze lumbered into the alley, blocking my path.

"Leave me alone!" I screamed. My voice came out high and shrill.

His oily face was set in a hard scowl. He didn't look friendly.

Black lumps oozed down his forehead, over his eyes, and down the sides of his face. He kept clenching and unclenching his huge hands into fists.

"I mean it! Leave me alone!" I cried. "I'll call the police! Really!"

I pulled my phone out of my pocket and held it up in front of me.

He waved his hand – and slapped it away. The phone hit the back wall of the Dairy Freeze. It broke into two pieces and dropped to the alley floor.

"What do you *want*? Leave me *alone*!" I screamed. "I don't have your stupid book!"

I squinted into the back window of the Dairy Freeze. Maybe one of the workers would hear my screams and come out to help me.

But no. I saw one girl scooping ice cream and another girl tapping on the till. They didn't turn around.

The Ooze bumped up to me. He reached out a gunky hand and rubbed it across my cheeks.

"Owww!" I let out a howl. "That BURNS!"

I reached up my hand. I had a thick smear of black gunk stuck to my face. I shook my head hard, trying to cool it down. It was burning hot!

I staggered back until I hit the rear wall of the Dairy Freeze. I turned quickly. Could I make a run for the street?

"Don't try it," The Ooze growled. "Why don't you just hand it over? You know what I came for."

24

"Wh-what do you want?" I stammered. "I *don't* know what it is. I told you—"

He leaned over me. He pressed a finger against one of his nostrils – and blew out of the other nostril. Hot oily gunk came shooting out of his nose and splashed on to the back of my neck.

"*Owww.* Sick!" I twisted and squirmed. I was pinned against the brick wall. No way to escape.

My heart was racing in my chest. The back of my neck throbbed with pain.

"D-don't blow your nose on me! I – I told you," I choked out. "I already told you. The book is gone. It was stolen by a man with fire all around him."

He stood straight up. I think that surprised him. I could see him thinking hard about it.

Then he leaned over me again. His dark eyes locked on mine. "I don't believe you," he growled.

"Know what I mean?"

"I – I'm telling the truth. Why would I lie?"

He stuck out a greasy hand. "Give it, kid. Now. Give me what I'm looking for – and maybe I'll let you live."

"Huh?" A gasp escaped my throat. "What are you talking about? *Tell* me! Please—"

He leaned closer. I choked on his thick tar smell. The heat off his body sent rivers of sweat down my face.

"You want to play innocent?" he boomed. "Sorry, kid. You give me no choice. *Know what I mean?*"

My mind was spinning. It was so hard to think. The bitter tar odour . . . the intense heat . . . the cold stare of his eyes. . .

"Sorry, kid." The skin on his face began to bubble and fizz. Oily black lumps rolled over his hands, his neck, his chest. "No more Mr Nice Guy."

I could see what he was going to do. No more hot oil drips. That was baby stuff.

I'd seen it in all the comic books. He was going to rise up three metres high, then splash down over me in a wave of oily sludge.

I tried to duck. Tried to dodge away.

But he had me trapped.

I'm going to be buried under it!

I'm going to drown in it!

Were those my last thoughts?

The bubbling, sizzling Ooze swept high over my head.

I shut my eyes. I held my breath.

I knew I had only seconds before he came crashing down on me.

Doomed. I was doomed.

Unless my big idea worked. The plan I'd thought about all night. . .

Destroy him before he destroyed me.

Well, this was definitely the time to try it!

25

"You don't scare me, Ooze!" I shouted at the top of my lungs over the roar of the sizzling goo.

The wave of burning tar stopped. Pulled back a little.

"I read the *Wizard of Ooze* book!" I shouted. "And now I have powers, too!"

The wave of oily gunk pulled back. The Ooze settled down to his original size and shape.

His big bubbly chest heaved in and out. His eyes bulged wide. His ugly mouth was open, and the blue tongue slicked from side to side.

"Powers?" he sneered. "What kind of powers do *you* have, punk? The power to scream like a baby?"

"Uh . . . my new name is TIDAL WAVE!" I cried. I'd thought of the name the night before.

He narrowed his eyes at me. His sharp teeth made a clicking sound as he chomped them up and down.

"I am Master of the Water Universe!" I

shouted.

Of course, my water powers lasted for only ten seconds, I thought to myself. *And I have no idea if I can even bring them back for another ten seconds.*

Maybe I can fake him out. I have to try!

The Ooze crossed his arms in front of him. The arms made a wet, squishy sound as he pulled them against his chest.

He stared hard. Didn't say a word.

"I found my powers in a freezing-cold bathtub," I said. "Maybe you've read that chapter."

He didn't move. Didn't blink.

"Well . . ." I continued. "Now I have the amazing strength and power of a tidal wave!"

The Ooze tossed back his huge head and let out a roaring laugh. When he finally finished laughing, he pressed his hands to his waist.

"Tidal Wave, huh?" he boomed. "You don't know anything about waves, punk. The only wave you know is how to wave bye-bye!"

He let out another roaring laugh. His breath swept over me, hot as if it came from an oven.

I stood still, hands clenched at my sides. I hoped he couldn't see how hard my legs were trembling.

He lowered his head and grinned a sick, toothy grin at me. "Let's see what you've got, punk. Go ahead. Show me something."

26

My brain did flip-flops in my head. I gazed all around.

No icy bathtub anywhere in sight. What could I do?

Try it anyway, I decided.

I shut my eyes and scrunched up my face, struggling to concentrate.

"You asked for it, Ooze!" I cried. "Now you will feel the power of Tidal Wave!"

"Do your best," he replied. "You'll need your best to fight me. *Know what I mean?*"

I shut my eyes tighter. I tried to force all thoughts from my mind.

I pictured the ocean. Dark blue waves. Miles and miles of dark blue water, as far as the eye could see.

Water . . . miles of water. . .

I pictured waves, rising high. Waves crashing against a sandy beach. Bright blue waves capped by frothy white foam.

Wave after wave sweeping on to a beach. I heard the crash of the water hitting the shore. The splash of wave crashing into wave.

My heart pounded so hard, I thought it was going to come flying out of my chest. I knew that any second The Ooze would come rolling over me.

I kept my eyes shut tight. I pictured the blue waves crashing ... crashing ... rising up and crashing.

"Oh." I gasped when I began to feel different.

My muscles squeezed tight. I felt my skin falling away.

Startled, I opened my eyes. I felt dizzy. My body swayed from side to side. I looked down. My body was changing ... dissolving ... melting.

I saw the shocked look on The Ooze's face. He couldn't hide his surprise. Bubbling hard, he took a big step back.

It's happening! I knew. *I still have the water power. Maybe once you have it, you have it for ever.*

I knew I didn't have time to think about it. I was water now. My body was a churning, frothy wave.

I pulled myself up. Swept high in front of the startled Ooze.

"Look out, Ooze!" I cried. My watery voice

bubbled from somewhere deep inside me. "Look out! Oil and water don't mix!"

Higher. I pulled myself higher.

I rose up over the wide-eyed supervillain. I began to roar. The roar of a powerful tidal wave.

Higher.

My watery body bubbled and frothed and bent. Ready to crash down over him.

"Hey, loser – feel the power of Tidal Wave!" I shouted.

And then it all went wrong.

27

Something popped.

I dropped hard to the pavement. Sharp pain shot up and down my body.

I looked down. I was me again. Solid. Normal me.

I pinched my chin. Skin – not water.

I was standing up to my ankles in a puddle of water.

Once again, the superpower lasted only ten seconds. What was I doing wrong?

The Ooze stuck out an oily finger and poked my chest. I felt a stab of heat through my shirt.

"You fool," he growled. "Do you really think this is a game for *amateurs*?"

He poked me again. "You lose, punk."

I took a step back. My shoes squished in the puddle. My fear tightened my chest. I could barely breathe.

"You – you're going to *ooze* me now?"

I choked out.

He rubbed his wet, oily chin. I could see he was thinking hard.

"I *should* ooze you," he said finally. "But I have to follow the Code of the Superpowers."

"Huh?" I stared up at him, trying to understand.

"The Code of the Superpowers," he repeated. "Since you have powers, I have to give you a second chance."

I swallowed hard. I couldn't believe my ears. Was he actually going to let me go?

He sighed. "It's the rule. Your powers last for only ten seconds. But I have to follow the code. So here's your second chance. . . "

He poked me in the chest again. "You said that The Fabulous Flame stole the Ooze book from you?"

"The Fabulous Flame?" I said. "You mean the guy who was on fire?"

He nodded again. "That's The Fabulous Flame. Actually, it's Sammy," The Ooze said. "You remember. The guy who worked for me in my booth at the comic convention."

My mouth dropped open. "Sammy is The Fabulous Flame?"

"Yeah. Sammy looks like a normal guy. But he isn't. He's a mutant."

The Ooze let out an angry growl. He smacked

his fist into his open palm. That sent gobs of goo flying in all directions.

"This is the *last time* he steals from me!" he boomed.

"I . . . don't understand," I said. "He works for you?"

"Yeah. I keep him around because I feel sorry for the guy," The Ooze said. "See, he's not as famous as me. He doesn't have his own comic or anything. But sometimes he gets jealous and does things to hurt me. Things I don't like."

He shook his head. "But *stealing* from me is going too far. I hate that guy. I really do."

"Then why do you keep him around?" I asked.

The Ooze scowled. "I have to be careful with the guy. He's fire, remember? He can burn me. He knows fire can burn oil. So I have to be careful with him."

"So what do you want me to do?" I asked.

The Ooze leaned close to me. "Put out his fire," he said.

28

I choked. It took me a few seconds to catch my breath. "Me? Put out his fire?"

"I can't do it," The Ooze said. "But you can. You can splash out his fire and grab the book for me."

I stared hard at him. He was serious.

The Ooze was giving me a chance to survive. All I had to do was destroy The Fabulous Flame for him.

No problem – right?

Then why were my legs shaking so hard and my teeth chattering like castanets?

"Splash out his fire and grab the book," The Ooze repeated. "It's simple. Anyone with water powers can do it. Get that book for me, kid. If you do, I have no choice. I have to follow the Code of the Superpowers. I have to let you go free."

"But . . . he could burn me to a crisp," I said.

My voice cracked. "I'm not sure—"

The Ooze's dark eyes narrowed into slits. His mouth tightened into a terrifying scowl. He began to bubble again.

With a whoosh of burning hot air, he rose up high. His shadow covered me in darkness. He leaned over me... leaned close till the heat scalded my skin.

And then he began to dip down, to spread himself over me.

"OK, OK!" I shouted. "I'll do it. Where do I find him?"

29

The Fabulous Flame didn't live in a furnace or a giant oven or anything. He had a normal-looking house about six blocks from the Dairy Freeze. I saw a small blue car in the driveway in front of the garage. And a leaf blower lying on its side near the front walk.

The Ooze and I crept up the driveway and made our way around the side of the house. "He fools people by living a normal life," The Ooze said softly. "Even his neighbours don't know he's The Flame. They just think he's Sammy."

My heart was pounding. My brain did flip-flops as I walked towards the back yard. Was there any possible way I could *survive* this?

"We need a plan," The Ooze muttered.

"Uh . . . well . . ." I cleared my throat. "I'll just tell him I recognized him when he grabbed my book," I said. "I'll tell him I'm his biggest fan. I'll . . . uh . . . ask him for his autograph."

"Good. You get up close to him. Then you splash him," The Ooze said. "Put out his fire. I'll grab the book."

Will my water power work? I wondered. *Maybe I didn't try hard enough before. Maybe it really is my superpower.*

In a few seconds, I would find out.

The Ooze gave me a hard shove into the back-yard. "Get to work, punk."

I saw Sammy. He was lying on a lounger on his patio. Did he see me? No.

I ducked back into the shadow of the house.

Sammy was sprawled on his back. He was bar-becuing a steak on his *flaming chest*! The steak sizzled and the flames jumped high.

Suddenly, he sat up. He saw me!

"Marco – what are you doing here?" The steak fell into his lap. Bright flames still danced from his bare chest.

I pointed at him. I pretended to be surprised. "I *knew* it!" I cried. "You're The Fabulous Flame – aren't you?"

He grinned. "I can't deny it." He set the steak down on a plate on a little table beside the lounge chair.

He jumped to his feet and started towards me. "What are you doing here, Marco? I hope you didn't come to get your book. Because I'm not giving it back."

"I . . . I don't care about that book," I said. "I'm your biggest fan! Really!"

He studied me. Flames popped up over the top of his head.

"I can't believe I'm standing here talking to The Fabulous Flame!" I cried.

I'm a good actor. I could see he was buying it.

"I can't believe you were in my room!" I gushed.

His grin grew wider. Flames darted from his arms and chest. "Did you bring what I'm looking for?"

"Yes," I lied. "I brought it. But first – can I have your autograph? I hope I'm not asking too much. But I would *love* to have your autograph!"

He motioned with a flaming hand. "Come sit down." He climbed on to the lounge chair and put the steak back on his chest. "How do you like your steak, Marco? Medium rare?"

"Uh . . . well. . ."

The flames leaped on his chest. As they shot up higher, they hid his face from me.

My chance to make my move.

I shut my eyes. I concentrated . . . concentrated. Again, I pictured blue waves crashing against a sandy beach. Frothing tall waves . . . roaring . . . crashing.

And a few seconds later, I could feel myself changing. I could feel my body melting away.

Feel my mind sinking into clear, cold water.

Yes!

Once again, I was Tidal Wave! My body had melted away. And in its place was a rushing, roaring tall wave of water.

I turned quickly. And *heaved* myself at The Fabulous Flame.

A powerful tidal wave, I swept over the lounge chair. Washed over it in a burst of water power.

I splashed to the patio stones. Started to climb up.

Ten seconds had passed. I was me again. Solid Marco. On my knees in a puddle of water.

And The Fabulous Flame?

He stood on the edge of the patio. He had his fiery hands at his waist. Flames swirled around his chest. I saw the steak on the ground next to the lounge chair.

"Too fast for you, Marco," he said softly. He glared at me angrily. "Nice try. But you lose, sonny."

He lowered his head. Then he came roaring at me, arms outstretched, a bolt of fire eager to wrap me in flames.

30

"Nooooo!" A terrified scream burst from my throat.

I tried to run – but I tripped over something. I went down hard on my knees. Turned and saw what I'd tripped over.

A garden hose.

I gripped it hard and struggled to stand up. My hand slid to the nozzle. I didn't even think about what I was doing. I just raised the nozzle, squeezed the handle –

– and sent a powerful spray of water at The Flame's chest.

He stopped in the middle of the patio. The flames swept back as if being blown by the wind.

I grabbed the hose with both hands and kept the stream of water on his body. I moved it up and down, from his fiery head down to his legs. Blasting him. Blasting him with a steady rush of water.

His arms shot straight out as the flames sizzled. They smoked and sizzled and faded.

"Heeyyyyyyyyy!" A wild cry escaped his throat as he toppled backwards. He landed hard on his back. The flames died. Smoke curled up from his chest. He didn't move.

"Good work, kid!" I heard a booming voice behind me.

I turned to see The Ooze come rumbling across the yard. He waved the book high in one hand. "Got it!" he cried. "Good work, Tidal Wave!"

I still gripped the nozzle tightly. I let go and the hose fell to the patio.

I was shaking. Totally in shock from my close call. "So . . . you've got the book," I said. My voice trembled. "Does that mean I can go free?"

"Of course not," he replied. "You know too much."

"But – but—" I stammered.

"It's a solid shame. A solid shame. But I have to ooze you, kid. Any last words?"

"Wait a minute!" I cried. "You can't! What about the Code of the Superpowers?"

"I made that up," the Ooze replied. "There's no such thing."

"But you said—"

"I was afraid you wouldn't cooperate," he said. "I thought you might try to escape or something. So I made up a stupid code. Big surprise, huh? I'm a *villain* – remember? *Know what I mean?*"

I stared up at him, shaking my head.

Once again, he began to bubble and grow. The heat poured off him as he rose up in front of me.

I spun away. I knew I couldn't outrun him.

Doomed. This was it. No more second chances.

And then a startled cry escaped my throat: "Gabriella? What are *you* doing here?"

31

Gabriella came running towards the patio. She wore a bright yellow T-shirt over black leggings. Her hair was tied back in a ponytail. It bobbed behind her as she ran. Her dark eyes were locked on The Ooze.

"No! Get away from here!" I shouted. "Run, Gabriella! You're in terrible danger here!"

She stopped. And stared up angrily at The Ooze.

"He's dangerous!" I screamed. "Get away from here!"

She lowered her gaze to me. "Marco, I read the book, too," she said. "Don't you remember? I read it in the car on the way home from HorrorLand."

"Yeah, I remember," I said. "So what? This is dangerous. You'd better—"

The Ooze leaned closer. I shuddered under his shadow.

Gabriella tossed her ponytail over her shoulder. "I tried the superpower chapters when I got home," she said.

I squinted at her. "You *what*?"

"I memorized them. I tried them," she said. "I mastered the power of the wind. And now . . . I call myself The Human Tornado!"

The Ooze let out a laugh. "Ooh, I'm scared! I'm *shaking*!"

"Gabriella – he – he's going to ooze me," I stammered. "Are you sure your powers —?"

"Watch me," she replied.

She shut her eyes and started to twirl on one leg. Faster . . . faster . . . until she was spinning so hard, she became a blur. A powerful blast of wind roared off her spinning body.

"Yes!" I cried. "Yes!"

The tornado winds blew my hair straight up. I staggered forwards – and almost flew right into The Ooze!

The patio chairs blew away. A table toppled over and skittered across the yard. Tree branches shivered and shook.

Gabriella spun harder. I could barely see her now. It was as if she had *become* the wind!

The Ooze raised both arms to shield himself. The powerful blasts of wind sent fat gobs of oily goo flying over the patio.

"Yes!" I shouted happily into the wind. "Keep

it up! Keep it up! You've got him, Gabriella!"

And then the wind stopped.

A horrible silence fell over the back yard.

Gabriella twirled on one leg ... slower ... slower ... until she toppled over – lost her balance and fell to the ground.

Ten seconds. The winds lasted only ten seconds.

Gabriella let out a groan. She lifted her head. "Uh-oh. I think I messed up."

The shadow of The Ooze fell over us both. He laughed again. "Did anyone feel a slight breeze?" he said. "How lame. Now I have no choice but to ooze both of you! *Know what I mean?*"

He began to bubble and grow.

Gabriella jumped up and came beside me. "Marco – run!"

Too late. He had us cornered against the back wall of the house.

He let out a furious roar – and a wave of hot air floated off his body. The air smelled foul, sour and thick as the stench from a skunk. Or maybe a *thousand* skunks!

I couldn't breathe. My eyes watered over. Gabriella and I began to gag and choke on the smell.

Another blast of hot wind. The Ooze stretched over us ... covered us in a terrifying darkness. Bubbling and fizzing ... he prepared to splash down.

My skin burned. I struggled to breathe. Wave after wave of the putrid odour attacked my nose.

"Ohhhhhhh."

Was that *me* moaning like that?

And then a flash of bright light burst through the darkness.

I turned my head. Blinking through my tears, I saw The Fabulous Flame. Burning again. Flames dancing all around him.

He came towards us, bright and fiery.

Covered in flickering flames, he strode up beside The Ooze.

The Ooze heaved himself back. Bubbling hard, he staggered away from the fire. A fast retreat.

"Where is it?" The Fabulous Flame shouted at me. "Where did you hide it, punk?"

I jabbed my finger at The Ooze. "He has it!" I cried. "*He* has the book!"

Flames shot off The Flame's head. "I'm not talking about the book!" he screamed. "You know what I want! Where is it?"

"Better hand it over to him," The Ooze boomed.

"I don't know what you're talking about!" I cried.

"Too bad," The Flame said. "You're going to

be *flamed* and *oozed* at the same time!"

Gabriella and I both screamed as they dived for us.

And over our screams, I heard a familiar voice:

"Is *this* what you're looking for?"

I spun to the side of the house. And let out a shout. "Zeke! What are YOU doing here?"

32

Zeke came running across the grass, waving something in his hand.

"Maybe *this* is what you want?" he cried. He flapped it back and forth.

The Ooze and The Fabulous Flame stepped back. They both stared hard at the object held tightly in Zeke's hand.

I didn't recognize it. "What *is* that?" I cried.

"The bookmark," Zeke said.

I squinted at it. "The *what*?"

"The bookmark from the Ooze book," Zeke said. "Don't you remember it? It has all these funny words on it. Didn't you read the tiny type? It says you have to say the words, or else your powers will last only ten seconds!"

Gabriella and I looked at each other. "That explains it," I said, sighing.

I turned to Zeke. "You – you've had the book-mark all this time?"

He nodded. "I took it out of the book. I thought it might come in handy sometime."

"Zeke!" I screamed. "Look at all the trouble you caused!"

He shrugged. "So?"

The Ooze held out his big oily hand. "Just give me the bookmark," he growled.

"We don't want it in the wrong hands – do we?" The Fabulous Flame added. "Those words will make my powers stronger."

"You mean OUR powers!" The Ooze boomed. "Give *me* the card, Zeke. The Flame can't be trusted."

"No way!" Zeke said.

"Give it to me!" The Ooze boomed. He made a furious swipe at it.

Zeke swung it out of his reach.

The Flame aimed a whirling fireball at Zeke's head.

Zeke ducked and the fireball flew over him.

"Too late! Too late!" Zeke cried. He did a crazy dance.

The Ooze and The Flame both dived at him.

But Zeke waved both hands. He made a hard sweeping motion.

And the two supervillains floated up into the air.

"Heeyyyyy!" The Ooze flapped his oily arms and thrashed his legs. "Put me down!"

"Put me down and I promise I won't hurt you too badly!" The Fabulous Flame shouted.

But Zeke waved his hands up again. He waved them high above his head.

And the two villains went flying . . . flying over the house . . . across the street . . . over the woods – flying higher and higher until they were tiny dots against the sky. And then they vanished completely.

Gabriella and I stood in shock, our eyes on the sky. Then we turned back to Zeke. He had a big victory grin on his face.

"My new identity is Lift-Off!" he cried. "I have antigravity powers."

"Wow! Very cool!" Gabriella cried. "You saved us!"

"That was amazing!" I exclaimed. "Good work, Zeke!"

"One wave of my hands and people go flying away for ever," Zeke said. "And my powers *last* because I'm not stupid like you. I read the words on the bookmark!"

I picked the Ooze book up off the patio. I rubbed some black gunk off the cover with my hand.

My heart was still pounding like a drum. But the two villains were gone. I knew I could finally relax.

"Everyone is in my power now!" Zeke cried. "Watch me send you flying into that tree!"

I grabbed his hand before he could raise it.

"Stop bragging and showing off," I said. "Let's go home and forget this ever happened!"

But, of course, I couldn't forget.

I wanted to be a real superhero, too.

I wasn't jealous of Zeke. I just didn't think he should be the only superhero in the family.

Besides, I didn't trust him. Sometimes he gets crazy and starts punching his pillow or ranting and raving. Sometimes he tries to get me in trouble.

I needed my own powers to protect myself. I needed to be Tidal Wave.

So the next afternoon I sneaked into Zeke's room. I searched everywhere for the bookmark with the secret words. *Where did he hide it?*

I pawed through every drawer in his dresser. I pulled out every book on his bookshelf. I looked under his bed. Under all the junk on his wardrobe floor.

I was sweating and breathing hard when I finally found it. I pulled the bookmark out from under his pillow.

I held it up to my face. My hand trembled as I started to read the words – the words that would make my tidal wave powers last.

"Hey!" I cried out as the bookmark flew out of my hands.

I made a wild grab for it. Missed. It floated up near the ceiling.

I spun around and saw Zeke in the bedroom doorway. He had one hand raised, making the bookmark float.

"Give it back to me, Zeke!" I shouted. "Drop it. Give it back to me – now!"

He shook his head. "No way, Marco. One superhero in this family is enough! And it's me. Me, me, ME!"

"You're a total jerk!" I said. "The book is mine. And the bookmark is mine. So give it back!"

"You want it?" he cried, stepping into the room. "You want it, Marco? Go *get* it!"

He waved both hands – and I felt myself lift off the floor. "Hey!"

He raised a hand – and I couldn't stop myself. He had me in his power. I was helpless. I floated all the way up to the ceiling.

"Put me down, Zeke!" I shouted. "I mean it. I—"

And that's when Mum and Dad walked in.

At first, they only saw Zeke. But then they glanced up and saw me floating on the ceiling, my arms spread like bird wings.

Dad uttered a cry of shock.

"Marco! What on EARTH is going on here?" Mum demanded.

"Uh . . . well. . ." My mind whirred. I gazed down at them.

"Uh. . . Would you believe this is an experiment for science class? This one's for *extra credit*!"

EPILOGUE

Zeke finally let me down. But first I had to *swear* I wouldn't go after the bookmark again.

So. OK. Whatever.

I don't have to be a superhero. I just have to be careful from now on to be extra-special nice to my brother.

I decided to tuck the *Wizard of Ooze* book away in a secret hiding place. There's a loose panel in the back of my wardrobe. I slid it off the wall and hid the book behind it.

At least now it won't cause any more trouble, I told myself.

I set the panel back in place. Then I turned to leave the wardrobe.

But something down on the floor caught my eye. A yellow-green glow.

Was something burning?

I bent down and picked it up. It took me a few seconds to recognize it. The little figure of a

HorrorLand Horror. The Horror that old guy in the gift shop attached to the wrapping on my book.

It glowed in my hand and felt warm.

As I stared, the glow spread. It grew brighter and filled the wardrobe with an eerie light. I tried to drop the Horror, but it clung to my hand.

And I could feel it pulling me . . . pulling me into the light . . . into the deep glow of the yellow-green light.

I heard a *whoosh*. Felt a blast of strong air against my body.

And there I was, blinking, shaking, unsteady on my feet. There I was, back in the old man's gift shop. Chiller House. Back in HorrorLand.

He stood behind the counter in his old-fashioned suit with the old-fashioned square spectacles perched on his nose.

And he grinned at me. Jonathan Chiller. His name came back to me. A gold tooth gleamed in his mouth as he smiled.

"Welcome back, Marco," he croaked. "Time to pay me back for your gift. Are you ready?"

"Ready?" I cried. "Ready for *what*?"

HorrorLand
(TRADING)
(CARDS)

WINNER TAIKALL

OCCUPATION: HorrorLand Game Creator and Professional Cheater

FAVORITE GAME: Pin the Tail on Your Sister

FAVORITE GAME IDEA: Sudden Death – with Real Death!

WORST GAME IDEA: Two-sided Dice

HORRORLAND SPLAT STATS

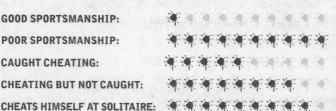

GOOD SPORTSMANSHIP:

POOR SPORTSMANSHIP:

CAUGHT CHEATING:

CHEATING BUT NOT CAUGHT:

CHEATS HIMSELF AT SOLITAIRE:

WINNER TAIKALL and his partner, BIG LOU ZERR, create all the games at HorrorLand. Their slogan: "It's not how well you play the game – it's how much you scream your head off." Their best games include: Grand Theft Tricycle, Battle Tetris, Tambourine Hero, and Madden 2011 Hopscotch.

Ready for More?

Marco is not the last kid to fall into Jonathan Chiller's trap. There will be six in all. Six who will "take a little Horror home with them". And then we will find out Chiller's evil plans.

Next up: you'll meet Ray Gordon, who has a terrifying adventure with Slappy the Living Dummy – in Goosebumps HorrorLand 18 – *Slappy New Year!*

When you read that book, maybe you'll take a little horror home with YOU!

Here's a chilling preview of:

I turned and gazed down the long, narrow aisle. I saw my reflection in mirror after mirror. Two rows of dark mirrors. A dozen Rays and Brandons. Maybe more, in front of us and behind us.

The dim light sent shadows over the glass. Our faces looked mysterious. Frightening. My eyes looked like deep, black holes. My mouth appeared jagged and torn.

I raised my right hand and watched the right hands go up in all the mirrors. I did a little dance, and the Ray reflections danced with me.

"What's so scary about this?" Brandon demanded. "What's the special part? It's just a bunch of mirrors. They aren't curved or twisted or anything."

"You're right," I said. I turned to him – and gasped. "Hey – where are you?"

"What do you mean, Ray?"

"I – I can't see you," I replied. My heart started to pound.

"Stop it, Ray," Brandon snapped. "You're not funny. I'm so sick of your dumb jokes."

"I'm not joking," I said. "Brandon, I really can't see you!"

"But I'm standing right next to you!" he cried.

About the Author

R.L. Stine's books are read all over the world. So far, his books have sold more than 300 million copies, making him one of the most popular children's authors in history. Besides Goosebumps, R.L. Stine has written the teen series Fear Street and the funny series Rotten School, as well as the Mostly Ghostly series, The Nightmare Room series, and the two-book thriller *Dangerous Girls*. R.L. Stine lives in New York with his wife, Jane, and Minnie, his King Charles spaniel. You can learn more about him at www.RLStine.com.

DOUBLE THE FRIGHT
ALL AT ONE SITE
www.scholastic.com/goosebumps
FIENDS OF GOOSEBUMPS &
GOOSEBUMPS HORRORLAND CAN:
PLAY GHOULISH GAMES!
CHAT WITH FELLOW FAN-ATICS!
WATCH CLIPS FROM SPINE-TINGLING DVDs!
EXPLORE CLASSIC BOOKS AND NEW TERROR-IFIC TITLES!
CHECK OUT THE GOOSEBUMPS HORRORLAND VIDEO GAME!
GET GOOSEBUMPS PHOTOSHOCK FOR THE iPHONE™
OR iPOD TOUCH®!
SCHOLASTIC
GBWEB

Goosebumps HorrorLand™

REVENGE OF THE LIVING DUMMY
R.L. STINE
SCHOLASTIC

CREEP FROM THE DEEP
R.L. STINE
SCHOLASTIC

MONSTER BLOOD FOR BREAKFAST!
R.L. STINE
SCHOLASTIC

THE SCREAM OF THE HAUNTED MASK
R.L. STINE
SCHOLASTIC

DR. MANIAC VS. ROBBY SCHWARTZ
R.L. STINE
SCHOLASTIC

WHO'S YOUR MUMMY?
R.L. STINE
SCHOLASTIC

MY FRIENDS CALL ME MONSTER
R.L. STINE
SCHOLASTIC

SAY CHEESE – AND DIE SCREAMING!
R.L. STINE
SCHOLASTIC

THE SCARIEST PLACE ON EARTH!

WELCOME TO CAMP SLITHER
R.L. STINE

HELP! WE HAVE STRANGE POWERS!
R.L. STINE

ESCAPE FROM HORRORLAND
R.L. STINE

THE STREETS OF PANIC PARK
R.L. STINE

WHEN THE GHOST DOG HOWLS
R.L. STINE

LITTLE SHOP OF HAMSTERS
R.L. STINE

HEADS, YOU LOSE!
R.L. STINE

WEIRDO HALLOWEEN
R.L. STINE

THE WIZARD OF OOZE
R.L. STINE

The Original Bone-Chilling

Goosebumps®

Series

—with Exclusive Author Interviews!